Other books by Paula Danziger

THE CAT ATE MY GYMSUIT
CAN YOU SUE YOUR PARENTS FOR
  MALPRACTICE?
IT'S AN AARDVARK-EAT-TURTLE
  WORLD
THE PISTACHIO PRESCRIPTION
REMEMBER ME TO HAROLD SQUARE
THERE'S A BAT IN BUNK FIVE
THIS PLACE HAS NO ATMOSPHERE

THE
DIVORCE EXPRESS

PAULA DANZIGER

THE
DIVORCE EXPRESS

The Putnam & Grosset Group

A PaperStar Book, published in 1998
by Penguin Putnam Books for Young Readers,
345 Hudson Street, New York, NY 10014.
PaperStar is a registered trademark of
The Putnam Berkley Group, Inc.
The PaperStar logo is a trademark of
The Putnam Berkley Group, Inc.
Originally published in 1982 by Delacorte Press.
Published simultaneously in Canada
Printed in the United States of America

Library of Congress Cataloging-in-Publication Data
Danziger, Paula 1944- The divorce express.
Summary: Resentful of her parents' divorce, a young girl
tries to accommodate herself to their new lives and
also find a place for herself. [1. Divorce—Fiction.
2. Parent and child—Fiction] I. Title.
PZ7.D2394Di 1982 [Fic]   82-70318
ISBN 0-698-11685-2
10 9 8 7 6 5 4 3 2 1

TO FRIENDS who have seen me through a writer's block, who have read this story or heard it over the phone, who have offered advice and friendship:

Nancy Kafka, Aviva Greenberg, June Foley, Annie Flanders, Rosie Flanders, Chris Flanders, Nicholas Nicholson, Melita Horvat Stupack, Michael Stupack, Sue Haven, Mark Haven, Paul Haven, Judy Gitenstein, Peter Bankers, Lila Browne, Ann Symons, John Symons, Joel Symons, Esther Fusco, Andrea Fusco, Chris Fusco, Andy Fusco, Max Lindenman, Barry Samuels, Maggie Denver, and Fran Weiss.

ALSO to the town and people of Woodstock.

You don't have to suffer to be a poet. Adolescence is enough suffering for anyone.

—John Ciardi

Rearrange the letters in the word PARENTS and you get the word ENTRAPS.

I found that out one day when I was playing Scrabble, got the seven-letter word and had no place to put it.

That's the way I'm feeling right now, trapped with no place to go.

It's not fair. A growing girl should have parents who act more like grown-ups. They're supposed to know what they want out of life and not be confused and constantly making a lot of changes.

Not my parents though. They are still, as my father likes to say, "getting their act together."

They started getting their act together by breaking up. That happened the summer I was between seventh and eighth grade. It was a real shock. Sure, I knew they weren't getting along well, but I didn't expect divorce. Not the way it happened.

Right after seventh grade I was sent to camp. My parents told me that camp would be good for me since I was an only child.

Good for me, ha! It was their chance. My father moved out.

I had no say. It was all arranged by the time I got home from camp.

My mother got to stay in our New York apartment and keep the furnishings.

My father sublet another apartment nearby and got the summer house in Woodstock.

Each of them got part of the savings.

My father got the car, which my mother had never learned to drive anyway.

Both of them got me, joint custody.

I lived half a week with one parent, the second half with the other. Weekends were alternated. If this sounds confusing, it was. I had to keep track of everything with a calendar. Once everything got really messed up. Each parent thought it was the other's weekend to have me, and both of them made plans to go away. It was awful. I felt like neither of them wanted me. Finally I ended up calling my friend Katie and making plans to stay with her. By that time both of my parents had canceled their weekend plans.

For all of eighth grade I commuted between the two apartments.

It was weird.

At my mother's I had my old bedroom. At my father's I slept on a convertible sofa bed.

During that time, the differences between my parents really showed. They should never have gotten married so young. They should never have had a kid. But they did.

I had two different wardrobes. My mother likes me to wear designer clothes, the ones with alligator, horse, and swan emblems. My father, however, is always buying me message T-shirts, like DON'T HASSLE THE HUMPBACK WHALES. It got so that my friends could tell which parent I was staying with by the clothes I was wearing.

My father really loves the country. He wants to paint and not work in an office for someone else.

My mother enjoys living in the city, loves being an interior decorator, and gets poison ivy from just looking at pictures of nature.

By the time that the divorce came through, the only thing they agreed on was that they should live in the same neighborhood so I wouldn't have any trouble getting to school.

I had no trouble getting to school. I just had trouble once I got to school.

Something happened to me after the separation and divorce.

They thought they had everything figured out just right. Only they didn't. They forgot that I might have feelings too.

So I did lots of things at school. I talked in class all the time, never turned in any homework, wouldn't give the right answers when teachers called on me.

One day I got to school real early and snuck in. I Krazy-Glued everything I could. In the men's faculty bathroom, I glued down the toilet seats. In the women's faculty room I plugged up the coin slot on the Tampax machine. In the science lab I glued everything in sight—chairs, the desks, the Bunsen burners. I even found the teacher's marking book and glued that to her chair, which I had already glued to the wall.

Then I went to homeroom.

It didn't take them long to figure out that something was wrong, since I'd also glued the lock to the front office. It also didn't take them long to find out who was responsible, because the tube had leaked and the fingers on my right hand were glued together.

The principal said she was shocked to "see a girl create such havoc."

I told her that with Women's Liberation anything was possible.

My parents really had to pay that time. They had to come in for meetings and then they had to pay for repairs. They're still taking money out of my allowance for that.

I was suspended for a week. When I got back, I talked to Ms. Fowler, the guidance counselor. She discussed it with me, asking if maybe I just wanted something in my life to stay in one place.

My parents started to see each other to talk about the problem—ME. For a while, I thought that maybe they'd even get back together.

They didn't.

While all of this was being discussed, other decisions were made. My mother decided to open up her own design business and would have to travel more.

My father decided to quit his job and take two years to live in the country, paint, and try to support himself as an artist.

Once again they decided what was "best" for me.

Now I'm living in Woodstock all week with my father and almost every weekend, I go down to New York City to be with my mother, riding the Divorce Express.

2

The Divorce Express. I don't have to board it this weekend because my mother's on a business trip. It's the bus that leaves Woodstock on Friday afternoons and returns on Sundays filled with kids who live with one parent in town and visit the other parent in New York City. It's really public transportation, but because of all the kids, it's nicknamed the Divorce Express.

Maybe not every place has a bus like it, but I know that there are other ways divorce kids travel to see parents. Planes. Cars. Trains. Subways. Cabs.

The transportation industry would be practically bankrupt if it weren't for divorce. A presidential candidate could run on the platform that divorce is good for the economy. Make it seem patriotic to have kids, then split up. He or she'd probably win—especially since kids don't vote.

This is my first weekend in Woodstock since school started and my father, the big game hunter who grew up in The Bronx, a part of New York City that is definitely not country, has just trapped a raccoon.

Not just any raccoon—my pet. At least I think of him that way. He came around a lot at night and even though he didn't eat out of my hand, he was getting close.

Some people may not think that's such a big deal, but it was to me. Ninth grade. A new school. All of my friends are back in New York City. I went away to summer camp again, so I didn't meet new kids here—the all-year-round ones. I've been in school a whole week and know no one, except to sort of nod hello. It's really rough. And I can't even have a cat or dog because my father's allergic. The only person I really know here is my father. It's all so different and kind of lonely. I really looked forward to the nights when the raccoon came around. He was my only friend, and now he's in a trap.

At least it's a Havahart trap, so that his whole body is inside, instead of just his paws. My father said he wouldn't use the other kind, where the paws get trapped and sometimes the animal chews off the paw to get out. But, any trap entraps. It's so gross, I can't stand it. I guess I should be thankful that he's not hurt, but my father is still planning to take him away.

"Phoebe, honey," my father says, motioning me to come over. "Look at it."

"He's got a name," I snarl. "It's Rocky. Let him go."

"Rocky keeps knocking over the garbage even when the lids are tied down. He's got to go." My father runs his hand over his head. That's a nervous habit he's developed since he's started going a little bald, like he's checking to make sure there's some left.

"Let's keep the garbage in the house," I say.

"Collection's only once a week. It'll stink."

Personally I think you stink, I want to say to him, but don't. Instead, I make another suggestion. "I'll pick the trash up every morning before school."

He shakes his head. "No. Last time you did that, you went back into the house and threw up from the smell."

The raccoon is beating his body against the cage, trying to get out.

"The only reason I threw up was because of the smelly yogurt containers. I'll wear a clothespin on my nose." I pick up a twig, refusing to look at my father.

The yogurt containers. I came back from camp to find out that my father's turned into a health nut—no red meat, almost no processed sugar, no cigarettes. Now our garbage is filled with healthy trash—granola boxes, bean sprout wrappers, mung bean and tofu leftovers.

My father's got that look on his face that means no fooling. "Phoebe, I'm taking Rocky over to Charlie in the morning and letting his dog sniff him, get the scent, and release him over there. He'll get away with a fighting chance."

I pick the bark from the twig. It's no use. The dog'll get Rocky's scent and then when it's hunting season, my raccoon will be a goner.

My father comes over and puts his arm around my shoulder.

I duck out from under it.

Rocky's still throwing his body at the side of the cage.

I think about a line from a poem my English teacher read to us in class last year: "I know why the caged bird sings." Then I miss New York City. New York, where you just dumped the garbage down the compactor and never thought about it. New York, where my best friend Katie lives. Where Andy, my boyfriend until I moved, still lives.

My father smiles. "Look, honey. The cage is made in Ossining, New York . . . the home of Sing Sing Prison."

Snapping the twig in half, I fail to see the humor.

He tries again. "Come on, Phoebe, he's got to go. Remember how he tore a hole in the screen door, got in, and practically destroyed the kitchen?"

It's dark by now. I can't see the trap but I can hear the banging noise.

"Tomorrow morning I'll take Rocky away and you and I will go some place special." My father tries to pat me on the shoulder.

I move away, throwing the pieces of twig on the ground.

Parents think they can bribe you into anything. Well, it's not true.

I pick up my flashlight and walk across the lawn, careful not to trip over the newly delivered firewood.

My father follows.

The banging noise continues.

Going in the front door of the house, I walk into the living room and look out the window at the Ashokan Reservoir. It's one of my favorite views, but tonight even that's not enough to calm me down. Nothing can.

I go into my bedroom, slam the door, and throw myself on the bed. I stare at the Sierra Club calendar that my father gave me and wonder how he can do this to Rocky if he cares so much about nature.

I'm never going to talk to him again.

There's knocking at my door. "Phoebe. Let's talk. Or play Scrabble with me. You know you love to play Scrabble."

DO NOT DISTURB says the sign that my father and I made up the time we worked out a system to allow each of us privacy. I open the door and put it on the outside knob, careful not to look at my father. Then I go back inside.

He yells, "I'm sorry, but we've got to do this. Rocky's a nuisance."

So are you, I think.

Finally I hear him go away.

I lie on my bed, on my side, staring at the picture my father painted of me sitting by the pool. He's so hard to understand. This move has really confused me. I don't even have a place to go if I run away. My friends in the city don't have that much room. Anyway their parents would tell on me. My mother would just send me back. She's too busy looking for perfect antiques for other people's houses. I could sneak out in the middle of the night and free Rocky, but my father'd never forgive me and I've got to live with him. There's no way to win.

Some days are just awful. This has been one of them.

3

The phone rings, awakening me.

I look at the clock. It's six thirty in the morning. There's no one who's going to call me at that time. It must be for the big game hunter. Let him get it.

The phone keeps ringing.

I put the pillow over my head.

Where is my father?

Why doesn't he get it?

The phone keeps ringing.

I reach for it.

It falls off the nightstand.

As I go to pick it up I yell, "Hold on. I'll be right there."

It's under the bed.

Finally I get it, making a sound that I hope passes for hello. Mornings are not my best time.

It's my father. At first I figure he's picked it up, finally. I listen to figure out what nitwit is calling at this hour.

The nitwit is my father.

"Phoebe, I'm over at the gas station. I took Rocky away this morning, early, so that you wouldn't have to deal with the situation. Listen, don't hang up on me. I've got something important to tell you."

I listen, saying nothing, twirling the phone cord.

"Are you still there?"

"Yup. I just got to sleep after worrying all night." Sometimes it's good to make a parent feel a little guilty.

There's a pause. "I didn't sleep well last night either. So about four o'clock this morning, I checked up on you. You were sound asleep," he answers.

Sometimes a parent likes to make a kid feel guilty too.

"We'll discuss all of that later," he says. "Right now though, we've got a problem."

I thought we already had a problem.

He continues. "Charlie says that Rocky's not a he, she's a she."

He woke me up to tell me that?

Sometimes he's very hard to understand.

I mumble something without really saying anything.

"She's a nursing mother," he says. "The babies will die if I don't bring her home. It's probably crazy, but I'm bringing her back. We'll get stuck with Rocky and her babies knocking over our garbage . . . but I just can't let them die."

I wake up. "Oh, Daddy. . . . Thank you."

He sighs. "We'll be home soon. Why don't you get breakfast going?"

"I'll make you the best breakfast ever." I want to hug him.

"See you soon," he says. "Phoebe, I love you."

"Me too—I love you too. I think you're wonderful," I gush.

"Look, honey, I'll be home in a few minutes. I'm just going to stop off for the Sunday paper."

After we hang up, I jump out of bed and get dressed, putting on my new jeans and sweat shirt, which I was saving for a special occasion.

The sweat shirt's a little tight, the way they always are when they're not broken in. Pulling it out, I try to stretch it.

That's one of the reasons that I need to have a best friend in Woodstock. That's what best friends do—help you stretch your sweat shirts . . . talk . . . have pimple-squeezing sessions.

I really miss Katie, my best friend in New York City. We used to do lots of things together, like the time we took five rolls of toilet paper and completely covered her older sister's room with it. And the time we roller-skated in the fountain in Central Park. We could also be serious. Like when my parents were getting a divorce and when her father found out he had cancer. We really helped each other through both of those things. Sometimes I want to slug the grown-ups who say that childhood is so easy and fun. It isn't.

I know that Rocky's not the answer. A raccoon can't do the things Katie and I used to do together, but at least having her around will make me feel better until I do make a friend.

I rush into the kitchen and start the breakfast—melon, peppermint tea, carrot juice, pumpkin bread, and an omelet—all things that I know my father loves.

When the car pulls up in the driveway, I rush out and hug my father.

We get the cage out of the car trunk.

Rocky's not moving much. I'd be pretty scared and tired, too, if I'd been through all that.

My father takes a stick to open the cage door. "Stand back, Phoebe. She may be angry. I don't want to have to take one of us to Kingston General Hospital with a raccoon bite."

The cage door opens.

We step back.

Rocky just sits there.

My father prods her with the stick.

Looking carefully at us, Rocky steps out.

She's so cute—those little paws, the way her face looks like she's a bandit with a mask.

She's not moving.

I kneel down and talk to her. "Go, Rocky. Go back to your babies."

"She's afraid to lead us to them. Let's go inside." My father takes the paper out of the car.

We start walking down the path, arm in arm.

I turn around.

Rocky's rushing off.

"Daddy, thank you." I pat his arm. "I promise to clean up the messes."

"I'm going to have a trash bin built." He sighs. "Then we won't have to worry. We should have done that from the beginning. I just didn't want to spend the money on it."

"We can leave some leftovers out for Rocky and her babies." I open the back door to the kitchen-dining area.

My father goes inside.

I follow.

He's talking to himself. "Full-time country living takes some getting used to. It's so different. I hope I made the right choice."

Me too, I think, making the omelet. Sometimes late at night I think about what it would be like if we could move back. But when I mentioned it, he got upset. So now I just think it, I don't say it.

I make the omelet while my father starts *The New York Times* crossword puzzle. Scrambling the eggs, I mix them with onions, mushrooms, pepper, and cheese.

Now that there are just the two of us, I do a lot of the cooking.

The breakfast's on the table. It looks great but I'd love to have bacon. My father's turned into a semi-veggie, so I have to wait till I go to New York for my meat fix.

My father tastes the food. "This is really good. Listen, there's a terrific band playing tonight at the Café Expresso. Let's go."

"I'd love to." It'll be like a date with my father.

"I'm going to spend the day painting. Mind making the dinner tonight? I'll be on food detail tomorrow."

"Leave it to me." I clear the table. "It's going to be a meal you'll never forget."

4

Whenever I cook, I think of Missy Mandelbaum. She was the only kid in the Shake, Bake, and Make elective back in my old school who got an A-plus. I wish she were here now to help me prepare this meal. It may turn into a dinner my father will never forget because it'll be the pits.

I'm not a fantastic cook—or even a good one. In fact, I'm a pretty lousy cook. I've been trying, but it's not easy.

Before the divorce I helped out in the kitchen, but helping out is not the same as making an entire meal.

How do people get complicated meals together, set the table, and smile at the same time?

I started out my cooking career after I returned from camp. Macaroni and cheese from the package was my first solo attempt. "Not bad," my father said, so I made it every night for three nights. "Boring," he said, so I made it the next time with tuna fish, thinking maybe he wouldn't notice that I was still using boxed macaroni and cheese.

He noticed. He also read the ingredients on the package.

"Enough" was his response.

Now I'm trying out new menus, but there have been several disasters, like the time the recipe said "Blend the salad" and I threw it in the blender. That night we had salad soup.

I want everything to be special tonight, to celebrate Rocky's release and going to the Café Expresso to listen to live music.

The main course is easy. Cheese fondue. The bread cubes are cut and the cheese is grated. All I have to do is melt the cheese down with some wine in the chafing dish. The vegetables are cut and ready to steam. The salad is made, tossed—not thrown in a blender.

It's the dessert that's driving me nuts. My father loves mocha Bavarian cream, even if he is trying to stay away from sweets. It should be easy to make. My mother never had any problems with it. The recipe calls for two tablespoons of strong coffee and heavy cream. I've used the beaters on it, but it looks pretty weird.

I put my finger in the mixture and lick it.

It tastes pretty weird.

Times like this (and other times), I miss my mother.

She's out of town on a job and left a number to call in case of emergencies.

This dessert is a disaster.

Disasters are emergencies.

Therefore I can call her.

I dial the number my mother's given me.

I ask the person who answers to please put my mother on the phone.

The voice that answered sounded southern. I sometimes wonder about the people my mother decorates for. What they look like . . . what their houses looked like before . . . what they look like after she's done. . . . Sometimes I resent the people because my mother has to meet with them when it's convenient for them— like on a weekend I'm supposed to spend with her.

Finally my mother comes to the phone. "Phoebe, what's wrong?"

"Hi, Mom," I say. "How are you?"

"Out of breath from running to get to this phone." She takes a deep breath. "Is everything all right? Are you okay? Has anything happened to your father?"

I realize that I'm probably going to be in deep trouble for making this call. "Mom, everything's okay. I'm sorry to bother you, but I'm trying to make mocha Bavarian cream and I'm having trouble. I need your help."

There's a long pause, a very long pause.

"Mom, you don't have to help me if you don't have time," I say.

"You shouldn't have called me at a client's home unless it was an emergency. I was frightened to death. You should be more responsible."

"I'm sorry."

There's another pause and then a sigh. "Okay, just don't do it again."

"I promise," I say. "And, Mom, I guess I just wanted to talk to you. I miss you."

As I say that, I realize it's true. I do miss her. Whenever I'm with one parent, even if I'm having fun, there are times when I miss the other one.

She calms down. "I know, but you should have called tonight at the hotel, not here. Use the emergency numbers just for that."

"I promise. Honest." Sometimes parents think they have to tell you something twelve times before it sinks in.

"Now, as long as you've already gotten me out of the consultation, tell me what the problem is with the recipe."

I explain. "I took out the coffee beans, ground them up, and put them in the cream and beat them. The mixture tastes awful, gritty and yucky, not the way it is when you make it."

She laughs. "Phoebe, you're supposed to make the coffee first and then put in two tablespoons of liquid. That's what went wrong."

No wonder.

I feel like a real airhead.

She keeps laughing.

That doesn't help.

Finally she stops and says, "Don't feel bad. It happens to all of us. When I first got married, I wanted to make your father a lemon meringue pie. The recipe said to beat the egg whites. I boiled the eggs first and tried to beat them. How was I supposed to know you were supposed to beat them raw? So don't feel bad."

We talk for a few minutes more, then she says, "I've got to go. They're trying to decide whether to furnish the rec room in Art Deco or Hi-tech. Every-time I do a job in the suburbs, I swear that I'll never do another."

The suburbs on a Sunday—I wonder if she's caught poison ivy yet.

We tell each other that we love each other and then hang up.

I remake the dessert, brewing the coffee first. This time it works.

The dinner's a success. My father loves it.

As we're eating dessert I tell him that I called my mother.

"How's Kathy doing?" he asks quietly.

"Fine. Busy. Working hard." I pour myself more milk. "She told me how to make the dessert right. I goofed it up at first."

He smiles. "She always was good in the kitchen. Except for a few early disasters."

"Like the lemon meringue? She told me about that."

He takes more dessert. "Did she tell you about the time I tried to make a meat loaf?"

"No. I think she was kind of busy."

"I put hard-boiled eggs in it."

"That sounds right to me," I say.

"Without taking the shells off first?"

"No wonder you gave up red meat."

"It was for your mother's twenty-third birthday. She was pregnant with you. It was my first attempt at making anything that wasn't barbecued. She was so good about it, smiled as she picked the shells out of her teeth."

"Sounds like it was fun in a weird way."

"It was." He sighs. "There were some really good times between your mother and me. It's a shame it changed."

I just sit still, folding my paper napkin into a tiny square.

He looks at me. "The good memories and the fact that we have you make it worthwhile, Phoebe."

I put the napkin down and pat him on the hand. "Maybe it could still work out if you both really tried."

"We really did try, honey. It was no one's fault. I married someone who fit right in with the way I was brought up. Only one day I realized I didn't want to live the way I was brought up. Look, let's not talk about it. I'll do the dishes. You better get changed if we're going to leave in half an hour. Thanks for the dinner. You did a great job."

I look down at my clothes. They've got mocha Bavarian cream and coffee grounds spattered all over. That's because I turned on the beaters before I put them into the mixture. Gunk all over my new clothes. Now I'll have to wash them before wearing them to school. That's okay though. New clothes always have to look used to look right.

While I'm changing I think about the marriage and the divorce. I do that a lot.

I wonder if I'll ever get used to it and it won't hurt so much.

I hope so.

5

I feel like I'm on a grown-up date with my father, sitting at a table and listening to the Betty McDonald Band.

School's tomorrow, but tonight I can stay up late. My father loves to celebrate things. Tonight it's because Rocky's free. Once, before the divorce, he wanted to celebrate the septic tank being cleaned out. My mother said it was ridiculous to make a big deal out of something like that, but my father insisted. Now that they're divorced though, I'm glad to celebrate anytime he wants to.

The band's wonderful.

A woman comes up to the table and puts her hand on my father's shoulder.

She coos, "Hi, Jim, how are you?"

I want to smack her hand off his shoulder. She

looks like she once was a cheerleader—the type that's ever so cute, always tossing her hair a certain way.

My father looks up at her and then stands up. "Hi, Martha. I'd like you to meet my daughter, Phoebe."

She sits down without even being invited. "Hello, Phoebe. What a sweet name for such a lovely-looking girl. Don't you just love your name?" She uses that yucky voice that some grown-ups have when they don't know how to talk to kids like real people.

I stare at the band. "My name is Phoebe Anna Brooks. My father chose the first name after Holden Caulfield's little sister in *The Catcher in the Rye*, his favorite book when he was a teen-ager. My mother picked the name Anna because she likes palindromes, words that are spelled the same front and backwards. If I were a boy they would have named me Babbling— Babbling Brooks."

She giggles and looks at my father. "Babbling Brooks. . . . She's so cute, Jim. She looks just like you."

"Excuse me, please." I stand up. "I have to go to the bathroom."

To barf, I want to add, but don't.

I go to the bathroom door. There's a sign on it that says REST ROOM. I'll never understand why they call it that. People don't go in there to rest.

Knocking first, I make sure no one's in there and then I go in and look at the mirror.

Why can't I be beautiful? I look so average— brown hair, brown eyes, too thin eyebrows. Boring. I must have gotten average genes from an ancestor. My mother's a beauty. That's what Duane, her boy-friend, always says. Although he's generally a nerd, he's right about her looks. And my father's nice-looking. It's a case of two positives making a negative.

I put on lipstick, Passion Pink Frost.

It doesn't help.

By the mirror on the wall, someone's written HOO HA—SIX O'CLOCK. It makes no sense, but there are lots of things that don't make any sense.

Oh, well, I guess it's time to go out.

I walk out and stand by the salad bar.

Maybe she's fallen in a hole somewhere.

She's even taken my seat, the one closest to my father.

I go up to the table, pull over the other chair, and sit on his left side.

While I pretend to listen to the music, I listen to their conversation.

She's saying, "There's a great group, the Marc Black Band, at the Lake over the weekend. I hope you'll be there, Jim. You're such a good dancer."

I want to stuff her head into the drum set.

"Maybe. It sounds like fun." My father touches his bald spot. "Next weekend Phoebe will be visiting her mother in the city. When she's here, I like to spend the time with her. I'll probably be there. Be sure to save a dance for me."

"As many as you want." She gets up.

Maybe by next weekend someone will break her legs.

After she leaves, I turn to my father, who says, "Phoebe, you could have been more polite."

"She got on my nerves."

He shakes his head. "She's a nice lady."

"How do you know her? How does she know you're a good dancer?"

He picks up his swizzle stick and keeps hitting it on the side of his glass. "I love to listen to live music. I love to dance. The Joyous Lake is the best nightclub to do that in town. I went there during the summer, while you were at camp. I go there some weekends. You go to school and have the chance to meet new people. I don't."

"Did you ever go out with Martha?" I take the swizzle stick out of his hand before the tapping drives me nuts.

"No. But who knows? I may. Listen. I'm thirty-eight years old. Single. I date. I have a right to go out. It may upset you, but I do go out. I just don't do it while you're home. We have enough to adjust to already with our new life."

"I like our new life just the way it is," I tell him. "We don't need anybody else."

He shakes his head but says nothing.

I bite my fingernail. "I just don't want you to bring home a wicked stepmother some day."

He rumples my hair. "Don't give me that Cinderella number."

I pick up my soda. "And no mean stepsisters. Promise."

"I promise."

He's really a good guy.

Anyway, I'm the one who's sitting here with him— not Martha or anyone else.

6

The alarm goes off.

6:00 A.M.

No one in the world should have to get out of bed at that hour—except maybe people who do terrible things and deserve awful punishment.

Whoever invented Snooz-Alarms deserves a medal. Hitting mine, I stop the noise and go back to sleep.

6:10 A.M.

I hit the lever again and sleep some more.

6:20 A.M.

6:30 A.M. Whoever invented Snooz-Alarms should be tortured. If I don't get up now, I'm never going to make it to the bus on time.

Jumping out of bed, I trip over the clothes I wore last night. Messiness comes easy to me.

I stumble to the bathroom, brush my teeth, wash my face, and run a comb through my hair.

Looking at myself in the bathroom mirror, I say, "Come on, Phoebe Brooks, get your act in gear. You've got to go to school even if you don't want to go."

The face in the mirror has hardly opened her eyes.

I throw on some clothes—undies, jeans, a sweater, socks, Nikes.

I'm dressed like almost every kid in the school, wearing the unofficial uniform of Joyce Kilmer Regional High School.

I hate looking like everyone else. But I've tried so I could fit in, have friends.

It doesn't seem to work. Anyway it doesn't make me happy.

I add a long pair of beaded American Indian earrings and wrap a scarf around my forehead.

That's more like it. Maybe I'll look weird to everyone, but I'll feel more like me.

I grab my books and a coat.

As I rush out the door I can hear my father in his bedroom, snoring.

The bus is getting ready to leave.

7:00 A.M. on the dot.

I just made it.

Plopping onto a seat, I think—buses. I'm so sick of them. I bet I spend half my life riding them.

Taking out my notebook, I try to figure it out . . .

Wow, that means that over three weeks of my life each year is spent riding buses.

TIME

○ <u>SCHOOL</u>

    Bus departs – 7:00am

    Arrives at school – 7:30am

    Departs from school – 2:45pm

    Arrives at home – 3:15pm

An hour a day – 180 days a year = 180 hours

<u>THE DIVORCE EXPRESS</u>

    2½ hours each way. Twice a weekend.

5 hours per weekend. Approximately

42 weekends. (Not counting times not

traveled due to mother's business trips,

illness, summer, time spent with mother) =

$$\begin{array}{r} 42 \\ \times 5 \\ \hline 210 \text{ hours} \end{array}$$

<u>OTHER</u>

    Buses taken in New York City – the

time between Port Authority Bus Station

and my mother's apartment; all the times

I use a bus to go to movies, to shop,

to see plays, to visit friends.

It probably adds up to another = 150 hours

$$\begin{array}{r} 180 \\ 210 \\ 150 \\ \hline 540 \text{ hours a year} \\ \times 60 \\ \hline 32400 \text{ min. a year} \\ \times 60 \\ \hline 1,944,000 \text{ seconds} \end{array}$$

$$22½ \text{ days a year}$$

$$\begin{array}{r} 22 \\ 24\overline{)540} \\ 48 \\ \hline 60 \\ 48 \\ \hline 12 \end{array}$$

$$\frac{12}{24} = \frac{1}{2}$$

MILEAGE

NEW YORK / WOODSTOCK
    90 miles each way = 180 miles round trip
                        x 42 weekends
                        ─────────
                        360
                        720
                        ─────────
            * 7560 miles per year

TO APARTMENT —
    5 miles each way = 10 miles round trip
                        x 42
                        ─────────
            * 420 miles per year

SCHOOL
    15 miles each way = 30 miles a day
                        180 days per year
                        ─────────
                        2400
                        30
                        ─────────
            * 5400 miles per year

OTHER WHILE IN NEW YORK —
    approximately * 200 miles
        7560
        420
        5400
        200
        ─────────
    * 13,580 miles per year on a bus *

And that's without counting snow, ice, bad driving conditions, gridlock, mechanical problems.

I bet it all adds up to about a month a year.

If it continues all through high school, that's a third of a year.

It's a shame I wasn't born with wheels instead of legs. That would have saved lots in transportation costs—and I could get a special kind of sunglasses with windshield wipers and a defroster attached.

Maybe I should add a bumper sticker to my rear end. Most vehicles in Woodstock seem to have messages on them, like ANIMALS ARE TO LOVE, NOT TO EAT. ABORTION IS A CIVIL RIGHT. RIGHT TO LIFE. I ♥ WOODSTOCK. I guess my license would be 13580 for the number of miles spent on a bus, and my bumper sticker would read HAVE PARENTS, WILL TRAVEL.

Giggling, I try to imagine the way I'd look, certainly not like a typical Kilmer student.

"I've never thought doing math was so much fun," a voice says. "Hey, I like your earrings and headband."

Looking up, I realize that it's the girl sitting next to me. I've seen her before, but we've never spoken. She always seemed surrounded by friends—not the school "in crowd," but by lots of different people.

I touch my earrings to remember which ones I put on. "Thanks."

"You're new, right?"

I put my notebook away. "Actually I'm old—fourteen—but new to the school."

She continues. "That wasn't really math homework, was it?"

"I was just trying to figure out the hours and miles I ride on buses. School. New York."

She takes out a makeup case. "I heard you ride the Divorce Express."

"You heard?" I didn't think anyone had even noticed me.

She applies a little bit of peach blush-on. "Woodstock's really a small town. Word gets around. I usually ride the bus, too, but haven't lately. My father's a musician and he's been on tour, so I haven't been going. I start next weekend."

"Maybe we can sit together next time." I blurt it out without thinking that maybe she's already got someone to sit with. What if she says no or makes some dumb excuse to get out of it?

"Great. It's been really boring, the times I had to go down there. A lot of kids our age who have ridden on the bus for years give it up by the time they're in high school. I used to sit with my best friend, Jenny, but she had to go live in New York full-time. There was a custody fight and her father won."

"I live with my father, too, but there was no custody fight. It just worked out that way." Even though I'm sorry about her friend leaving, I kind of hope that she's got an opening for the position of new best friend.

"I bet that the math comes to about three full weeks a year, day and night. Right?" She applies some lip gloss from a round container. "Next you should try to figure out how much money the whole thing costs. It'll blow your mind. It's probably enough to put us through college, at least part of it."

I hadn't even thought of that. Bus tickets. Bus tokens. School taxes. I don't know what I want to be eventually, but I do know that I want to go to college. That's a lot of money.

She hands me the lip gloss. "Want to try this? It's new. Just got it."

I take it from her and put some on. It's strawberry, not my favorite flavor, but who cares?

Handing it back, I take a good look. She's wearing a red sweat shirt–like top, red sweat pants, black-and-red cowboy boots, and a glittered shawl. She's about my size, a seven, but she looks a little taller than me, about five seven.

"Your outfit looks great too," I say, meaning it.

"Thanks." She shows me that she has two pierced-ear earrings on one side and four on the other. "I like looking different."

"I was going to wear a feathered boa," I say, "but didn't think it would quite go at Kilmer."

"Feathers aren't in this year. You can't put designer labels on them." She shakes her head.

"My mother would love it here," I say. "She's into labels and names written all over clothes. Sometimes I think she looks like alphabet soup." I make a face.

"Not my mother. She loves to shop in thrift shops and flea markets," she says.

It's been so long since I've had someone my own age to talk to. "You've got a great tan. Did you get it over the summer?" I ask.

"Neither. My mother's white. My father's black. I'm a natural tan."

I wonder if anyone's ever thrown themself out of the school bus window because they've embarrassed themselves by dumbness.

Before I have the chance to open the window, she says, "If I'd lived in the South, back in the old days before the 1960s, I wouldn't have known where to sit on a bus."

I stand up and look to the front and then the back of the bus. "We seem to be in the right place, here in the middle."

"You're all right," she says as I sit down. "Why don't you sit with me and my friends at lunch? By the way, my name's Rosie. What's yours?"

"Phoebe." I want to stand up and cheer. "I'd love to. I was getting sick of spending the whole time hiding out in the bathroom. I was afraid that I'd die of smoke pollution there."

"The bathroom's a rotten place to spend lunch, though I'm not sure the cafeteria's any more appetizing. Sometimes it seems like they have the same stuff in both places. School lunches are a real waste."

"Gross. The lunches . . . and so's your pun." I grin to show her that I really like it.

"Wait till you taste the food."

The bus pulls up at the school.

We get off together and walk outside.

Maybe this is going to be a good school year after all.

7

One week I'm miserable. The next week everything's great. It's really weird how things happen. There are times I feel as if my heart is on a yo-yo.

Friday afternoon. Fifteen minutes to pack my bags. I should have done it last night, but first there was homework, and then Rosie and I talked on the phone for about forty-five minutes. We've been doing that ever since we met. One of the pains about living in Woodstock is that it's hard to visit friends without having your parents driving you there and picking you up. My father's obsessed with this painting he's working on, so I haven't wanted to ask him. Rosie's mother has to work every night, since it's still tourist season.

My father knocks at the door and says, "Phoebe, hurry up. You don't want to miss the bus."

I throw some stuff in my luggage. Books. Makeup. My favorite jeans. The football jersey that says WOOD-STOCK. COLONY OF THE ARTS. There's not much to take, since I have things at the apartment.

I rush out to the car. Standing by it, my father says, "Look at the way the leaves are turning color. I've been so busy working that I haven't really looked. Every year it starts and every year I'm stunned by the beauty."

He's right. Reds. Yellow. Oranges. Different shades of green. It makes me feel like I'm living in a kaleido-scope.

"It's a shame you can't stay this weekend. We could drive all over looking at the trees." He puts his hand on my shoulder, sounding kind of lonely.

"Do you have plans this weekend?" I ask, not sure if I want to know.

He shrugs. "I think I'm just going to paint."

Part of me would love to stay. The other part wants to go to New York City, to see Mom and Andy and Katie and the rest of the old gang.

Finally he says, "We better go."

I throw my bags into the car and sit down. "When I come back Sunday night, let's go out to dinner."

"After a weekend of cooking for myself, that'll be great."

We drive into town, over winding roads. Living in the Catskill Mountains means not having a lot of flat roads.

Going over Tannery Brook Road, we enter the town. Since there is really only one main street in

Woodstock, Tinker Street, that's where most of the action is, especially in the summer and fall months.

There are scads of people on the street. A lot of tourists. Summer people. Greens people (the ones who sit on the Village Green playing music and hanging out). The Orange people (who belong to some religious group that says they should only wear orange— and now cranberry—they own some sort of religious center nearby). Zen Buddhists, who also have a center. Regular Woodstockers, who become outnumbered by the summer people and tourists.

We park the car behind Houst's Hardware store. It's so hard to find a parking space with all of these people. Now that I'm a full-time Woodstocker, I can see why some of them resent the tourists and summer people, although they bring in lots of money.

We walk out through the alley. The town's so pretty—the little shops; a lot of them look like they must have when the village was first built.

Rosie's already waiting. She rushes over. "The bus is going to be late again. We've got about a half an hour to kill."

"Not again." I move out of the way of a tourist family who are trying to walk next to each other on the narrow sidewalks. "Rosie, this is my father."

"I've heard so much about you," they say at the same time.

Rosie puts her arm around a woman who has walked over to us. "This is my mother."

Rosie's mother's so beautiful. Long blond hair. Blue-violet eyes. Wearing a long patchwork skirt and leotard top, she looks like a model, except I know she's not. Rosie told me she's working as a waitress to earn money while she's trying to write a children's book.

Our parents shake hands and introduce themselves.

"Jim."

"Mindy."

A guy with a camera around his neck comes up. He's wearing plaid shorts and a striped top. "Could you please tell us where the Woodstock Rock Festival was held?"

Mindy explains that the festival never was really held in or near town, that the community didn't want it, so it was held on some pig farm in Bethel.

The man thanks her and walks over to the Village Green to take pictures.

I say, "I'd better call Mom and tell her I'm going to be late, not to worry."

My father says, "I'll give her a call later."

Rosie's mother frowns. "You'd better call your father, Rosie. I think that either he or his wife will be home. And remind him that his check is overdue, that I haven't received it yet."

Rosie looks at me and crosses her eyes, careful that only I see.

I know that the three of them—her father, her mother, and her stepmother—don't get along.

"Look," says Rosie. "You don't have to wait. I'll call New York, and then Phoebe and I'll go to the Laughing Bear Batik. I want to see if the shirt I love has gone on sale yet."

"Okay, just don't miss the bus," the parents say, almost in stereo.

Rosie and I kiss our parents good-bye.

"Nice meeting you," we say to each other's parents, and leave.

We go into the News Shop to use the pay phone. Since it's also the bus station, there are lots of different types of people sitting around. Most of the ones having coffee and something to eat at the counter are regulars. The people at the tables are sitting there with luggage, waiting for the bus, and reading, talking, eating.

In the back a few people are checking out the rack of newspapers and magazines. I recognize two boys from school who are sneaking looks at *Playboy*.

Rosie calls her father.

I try to reach my mother but she's not home.

We walk through the crowd and head to the Laughing Bear.

We go inside. On the left side of the store is Jarita's Florist; the clothes are on the right. There's no wall separating the two little shops. That makes it nice, a little crowded but nice.

We sort of walk in sideways. It's small and crowded with people. The clothes are all different colors, dyed and batiked. One year I bought Katie's birthday present here—a pair of pajamas with feet, decorated with stars, moons, and rainbows.

Rosie finds the shirt she wants. It still hasn't gone on sale. It's wonderful. Lavender with a unicorn batiked on it.

"Darn it." Rosie sighs.

So do I. I'd love to buy it, too, but it's more money than I can afford, especially since I'm still paying off the Krazy Glue incident.

The saleswoman walks up to Rosie and puts her arm around her shoulder. "I try to keep the shirt on the bottom so people don't see it right away. The sale on summer stuff should start in a few weeks. Maybe it'll still be here then."

I come up with a solution. "Let's pool our money, buy it together, and share the shirt. We can alternate weeks, or you can wear the back and I'll wear the front."

"No way. I may want to be liberated, but there's no way I'm going to walk around with a frontless shirt." Rosie smiles.

"Somehow I knew that." I pick up the shirt. "So what do you think? We'll buy it. You saw it first, so you wear it first. Take it this week."

The saleswoman says, "Why not flip a coin? That's what a lot of kids who share purchases do. I'll flip. You call."

Heads. I win.

We pay for the shirt. The saleswoman takes a penny off the price of the shirt so it comes out even.

As we leave the store I say, "I'll wear it when I see Andy this weekend. Then I'll wash it and give it to you so you can be the first person to wear it to school."

The bus arrives.

We rush, getting in line.

The line's not too long. Most people don't want to

leave Woodstock when the leaves are turning. There'll be more people coming in this weekend and more leaving on Sunday.

Mostly kids are in line, about ten of them. There's a little girl of about four holding on to her brother's hand. He's about seven. Two junior high girls are trying to finish their ice-cream cones before they enter the bus, and the driver tells them to throw them away. I recognize one or two kids from our school. Rosie was right though. We're among the oldest on the Divorce Express. Some of the older kids drive in themselves.

Rosie and I sit together.

With all of the kids on the bus it's like a school trip.

The bus driver announces, "Cigarette smoking is allowed in the last four rows. There will be no smoking on this bus of any other substances, legal or illegal."

The driver pulls out, careful not to hit any of the crowds crossing the street.

I wonder how my grandmother would have reacted to the driver's announcement. I hope, if she ever comes up to visit, she takes the train, even though it would be a half hour drive to pick her up.

All the way to New York, Rosie and I talk about our weekend plans. I'm so excited about seeing Andy, Katie, and the other kids. It seems like forever. And none of us has called the other since we last saw each other two weeks ago. I was so busy with all the new kids this week. Last time I saw the New York kids, they kept talking about all the work they had at the private school I used to go to. They kept making jokes about teachers I never had.

Rosie's excited because her father's playing tenor sax at a club and she's going to hear him.

Two and a half hours later we go through the Lincoln Tunnel. It's crazy, but we have to go through New Jersey to get to New York City. Even though I know it will never happen, I'm always afraid that the tunnel's going to spring a leak.

The bus goes over some of the dirtier New York streets and pulls into the Port Authority building.

Everyone starts pulling luggage and bags off the overhead racks.

Outside some start to line up by the side of the bus, waiting for the driver to open the compartments that store the larger luggage.

Finally Rosie and I get out.

Lots of parents are waiting to pick up the little kids.

We walk through Port Authority. Crowds of people coming and going from buses. Waiting in lines. Sitting on chairs. Some of the people aren't even going anyplace. They just hang out. Bag ladies, carting all of their possessions in shopping bags or carts. There's one guy who's going through garbage cans, looking for something to eat. Cops patrolling. People selling flowers. Some little kid crying because his mother won't buy him a pretzel. I wish they'd finish rebuilding this place. There are sections that are really nice, but I have to use one of the cruddy old sections.

Rosie rushes off to catch a subway train to Greenwich Village.

I get outside.

Fresh air. Well, at least semifresh air. Well, at least it's air.

I take two buses to get to Mom's Upper East Side apartment. The bus on the East Side is very different from the one on the West Side. Actually the buses aren't different, just the people. It's hard to explain. You see a lot more people wearing initial clothes on the East Side—the alphabet-soup gang.

I have to stand, the bus is so crowded. My bag keeps hitting the person standing next to me.

Finally I get off at my stop.

Wilbur, the doorman, is on duty. He's my favorite. I've known him since I was a little kid. He's always been real nice to me, sort of like a grandfather. Both of mine died before I was born, so he's the closest thing. Once I told that to Grandmother Brooks, and she said, "Ridiculous. How inappropriate to think of a common doorman as a grandfather of yours."

I'm glad that I hardly ever see her much. Since she's moved to Florida, all we usually get are letters and phone calls.

Wilbur opens the door. "Hi, Phoebe. How's it going? Glued any desks down lately?"

I put down my suitcase and stop. "No more. It caused too sticky a situation. I've reformed."

He groans, and I say, "How's it going with you?"

"I can't complain. The missus and I just got back from a vacation. We visited our daughter and her kids in Spirit Lake, Iowa."

It's kind of weird to think of Wilbur having a life outside the apartment lobby.

Looking around to make sure that no one can hear him, he whispers, "People in this building are really fighting, now that there's talk about going co-op."

Going co-op. That means that apartments that were rented may now have to be bought, like houses, with maintenance fees instead of rent payments. The owners will also have to pay mortgages. My mother likes the idea, thinks it would be a good investment as long as her business continues to do well. I worry though that some people may be evicted, especially some of the poorer people and some of the older people on fixed incomes.

He shakes his head. "Neighbors yelling at neighbors. I've never seen the building like this. People not speaking to each other, pretending that they don't see each other. I like New York better whenever there's an emergency, like a power failure. At least then, the people band together and aid each other."

I think about Woodstock and how whenever there's a problem, people hold benefits, auctions, and concerts and help each other out.

He says, "You better go up now. Your mother's called down here twice to see if you've arrived. I'll call her on the intercom and tell her that you're on your way."

I pick up my bag and wave good-bye as I hear Wilbur say, "Mrs. Brooks, your pride and joy is on the way up."

Oscar, the mean elevator man, is on duty so I don't

say a word to him. The only time he's nice is around Christmas, when it's time for tips.

My mother's waiting for me, with the door open. We hug.

She hugs me so tight, I feel like my ribs are going to break. It's nice being loved, but I hate to be bruised.

When she lets go, I kiss her on the cheek, walk in, drop my bag in the foyer, and head for the kitchen. "I'm starved. What's to eat?"

"I stocked up with all your favorite snacks. But first please put your bag away. Does your father let you leave a mess?"

Parents.

I put the bag in my room and then we sit down and talk.

As my mother tells me about her latest client, some guy who wants his Fifth Avenue apartment redecorated after his divorce, I notice that her hair's getting grayer. It's weird to think about parents getting older.

I tell her about Rosie and how I'm starting to make new friends. I don't mention how wonderful Woodstock looks with the leaves starting to turn colors. That was the only time she liked it up there, except for when she went antiquing.

Protecting parents' feelings can be a full-time job.

She tells me of all her plans for the weekend—dinner tonight, then a movie. Clothes shopping tomorrow and then a matinee. She knows I want to go to a party tomorrow night, so she'll go out with Duane, this guy she's been dating since she redid his office. He doesn't impress me, to say the least. In fact,

I think he's a real creep. He's the kind of guy who donates money to educational TV but watches football games—and that's one of his better qualities.

My mother continues telling me what we're going to do. Sunday brunch, and then she'll make me an early dinner before I have to catch the bus.

"Great," I say, wondering when I'm going to have time to do my homework and not sure that I should tell her that my father and I have made dinner plans for Sunday.

Before the divorce, and even when they both lived in New York, I had more time to do nothing with them. Now it all seems so busy.

Oh, well, it'll all work out. I'll talk to Andy and Katie and then I can let my mother know if I have to change some plans.

I go into my bedroom and call Andy. The line's busy.

I call Katie. Her line's busy too.

Taking the picture off my dresser, I sit down and look at it.

It's Andy and me on the school trip to Bear Mountain.

Andy's so cute—brown hair, brown eyes. He's getting so tall. Over the summer he must have grown about three inches. When we used to slow-dance, I could put my head on his shoulder. Now it'll be kind of under his armpit.

He's also really smart, nice, and a good kisser. It's a shame we didn't start going out until near the end of the school year.

I can't wait to see him.

8

I finally got through to Katie and almost wish I hadn't.

I'm not sure what to do or feel.

Katie and Andy have started going out together.

The conversation started out normally. How's school? What are you wearing to the party? Any good gossip? All the questions that I normally ask.

Then she said, "Listen, Phoebe, I don't know how to tell you this. . . ." And then she told me.

I hung up on her.

She called right back, but I told my mother to say I just left.

When I get upset or angry, I need time to figure things out or I say things I don't always mean, that I may regret later.

What choices do I have?

Do I tell them what creeps they are, what louses, traitors, cruds that are lower than earthworms? No— because they really aren't like that. They've always been my friends because they're wonderful people.

Should I go to the party, pretend I don't know them, and flirt with Charlie Shaw, who's had a crush on me since second grade? No—I do know them, and it's not fair to Charlie, who's a nice kid but not my type.

Should I try to find an excuse—like Andy's only going out with her because she's a real slime queen? She isn't. She doesn't. She has the same standards I do.

Should I rant and rave and carry on, sob that my life is over and no one's ever going to go with me again? No—that's not my style.

I'm not even sure of what I feel. I'm glad that *ambivalent* was on the English vocabulary list last week. It means having different feelings about the same thing. I guess that's the way it is for me. I like them both and think they'll be good for each other. Katie's been my friend since kindergarten. Andy was only my boyfriend for a couple of months. Part of me, though, also wants to wring their necks. Another part of my New York life is changing. But that's the way it's got to be because now I have to face the truth. Woodstock is the place where I have to make a new life. Thank goodness for Rosie.

What should I say to them? How should I handle this? Life certainly gets complicated. I guess that I'll have to take it all as it comes.

The phone rings again.

My mother comes to my door. "Honey, it's Andy. Is everything all right?"

I shrug and debate whether to take the call. "I guess I'll live. I'll take the call. Please hang up the phone in the other room. I'll take it in here."

Andy starts to explain right away, how they both missed me a lot and spent lots of time talking about me when school first started. Then they both were elected homeroom representatives and spent even more time together.

I just listen, saying nothing except "Uh-huh."

He continues. "It's hard with you gone. I want to go out and do things, and you're not here. My parents kept yelling about my calling you, that the phone bill would be too high. It gets lonely and boring, and Katie's a nice person—like you."

I say, "I guess it was kind of dumb to promise not to see other people."

"It just doesn't work long-distance, but I hope we can always be friends."

"Sure. Me too," I say, and realize it's true. We're only fourteen years old. It's just the beginning. And I think that one of the reasons I didn't make friends in Woodstock when school first started was because I gave off bad vibes about being there. Part of me really wasn't there.

After we hang up, I think for a minute, then pick up the phone to call Katie. A friend of my mother's once said, after the divorce, that relationships with men may not always last but that a good friendship between women is like gold. I'm not sure if my mother agreed, but I thought about it a lot.

Katie and I talk for about five minutes. We both cry a little, but I think it's more from relief than sadness.

She asks me if I'm still going to the party, that all the kids want to see me.

That would be too hard. I couldn't stand having everyone look at the three of us and think, Poor Phoebe. "My mother and Duane want me to go out with them," I say, hoping it was true. "They're going to a play. I'll see you all the next weekend I come down."

I feel grown-up after the talks, like I can handle anything. I think that kids who have gone through divorces are more used to handling problems. Maybe kids who haven't would disagree, but that's my opinion.

I think of a greeting card that I sent my mother once from the Woodstock Framing Gallery. It was when the divorce thing got really heavy. She still keeps it on the mantelpiece. It says WHEN THE GOING GETS TOUGH . . . THE TOUGH GO SHOPPING.

I walk out to the living room where my mother's waiting to find out what's going on and say, "Tomorrow let's use your credit cards and hit the stores."

She looks at me for a minute like I'm off the wall or something. I usually don't like to go with her, since our tastes are so different.

I point to the mantelpiece. "The card, remember."

It dawns on her. She walks over and hugs me. "I

only hope that whatever this is can be cured with an outfit, not a whole wardrobe."

I rub my head on her shoulder as she strokes my hair. "I think so."

It's kind of funny. I know that shopping doesn't take away bad feelings. It's just a symbol for keeping on with life.

It won't be so bad though to get some new clothes out of this. Maybe she'll feel so sorry for me, she won't bug me about buying stuff I don't want to wear.

Only forty-eight hours till I'm back in Woodstock.

9

"How was your weekend?" Rosie asks when I sit down next to her on the bus returning to Woodstock.

She doesn't realize what she's getting into. I tell her all about Katie and Andy. About buying a pair of boots. How when my mother realized I wasn't going to the party, she called Duane, who tried to get an extra ticket to the play, but they were all sold out. How Duane and my mother said they wouldn't go, but I told them to. How she called during the intermission to make sure I was all right. How I stayed in my room and cried a little, then took the picture of Andy and me and went out into the hall and threw it into the compactor and then felt bad that I did that.

"I feel better now. I think I've worked it all out of

my system. And they still are my friends. They both called and wanted to stop by, but I already had plans."

"Wow, I would have ripped off their faces." Rosie shakes her head. "I can't believe that you didn't scream at them, mangle their bodies into tiny pieces, and throw them to the rats to gnaw. That's what I would have done."

"What if the rats are veggies?" The thought of cannibal rats makes me ill.

"They're not. Those rats'd probably even eat cafeteria food," Rosie says. "I think you're being a regular saint about Katie and Andy. I wouldn't earn a halo on this one."

I make a mental note never to go out with anyone she's involved with, not that I ever would.

"You must have been really angry and hurt. Confess, weren't you?"

Thinking first, I say, "No. I really do like them both. Maybe if Andy were my first boyfriend, it would have been different. But he wasn't. My first boyfriend was Danny O'Hara in the fourth grade. We went steady until he traded me to Arnold Berman for one of those electronic toys. That time I got really angry. I tried to put Silly Putty up his nose until the teacher stopped me from doing something dangerous."

Rosie starts laughing and then I start.

People look at us and then turn away.

We keep looking at each other and laughing. We're all the way to Paramus, New Jersey, before we calm down. After the weekend I've just been through, it feels good to laugh.

"How was your weekend?" I ask.

"Fair. Listening to my father play was great. I'm so proud of him. But it's not easy. My father's new wife has two kids from her first marriage. They're seven and five, and they call *my* father Daddy. Sometimes they're brats, but mostly they're pretty okay. It's kind of weird though, like they're a full-time family and I'm a part-time visitor."

"That must be hard," I say.

She nods. "And I'm a lighter color than any of them. It's okay, but sometimes it makes me feel a little strange."

I think about what it must be like for her. I think she's wonderful and has everything going for her, so she should have no problems. But I guess everyone has some.

We turn the lights on over our seats to get some homework done.

A little kid in front of us, Stevie, is bus-sick. There's no parent with him, so one of the older kids, who's also alone, helps him.

There's a couple halfway back in the bus who are making out like crazy.

Finally the bus driver blinks the lights on and off to let them know they have to stop.

Doing homework under these conditions isn't easy, but it's the only real choice.

Two hours and then the bus pulls into Woodstock.

My father's standing there, waiting for me.

So's Rosie's mother.

We pile out of the bus and hug our parents.

"Want to go for pizza?" my father asks.

I think of the big dinner that my mother made, but that was hours ago. "Sure."

"Want to join us?" he asks Rosie and Mindy.

They accept.

We walk across the Green. It's much less crowded. Most of the tourists have gone. There are still some street people playing music.

My father takes my suitcase from me.

We go inside and get the little round table by the window.

My father pretends to take orders like a waiter. He goes back to the counter and places the order and then comes back and looks at the bulletin board, where the standings of the baseball teams are listed. Lots of the men in town play. It's a really big thing. My father says that when he gets to know more people, he'll join next summer.

When he comes back to us, I'm showing Mindy and Rosie my new boots, which are red and knee-high.

He sits down. "Your mother got those for you, I take it."

I nod.

"Are they lined?"

"No."

He shakes his head. "Winters get cold up here. Wouldn't lined ones have been more practical? At least these don't have initials. Sometimes I wish Kathy thought more. We'll still have to get boots that will work up here."

I wish I'd left them in New York, but then my mother would have felt bad.

Mindy says, "Sometimes it's nice to have something that may not be practical but just makes you feel good when you wear it. I have a hand-quilted vest like that."

Everyone gets very quiet at the table. I hope this doesn't turn into a disaster because my mother's bought me an expensive pair of boots.

The guy in the back yells out that our order is ready.

"Come on, Jim. Let's wait on our kids." Mindy gets up. "I'll help carry it. I'm not a stranger to waiting on tables."

My father and she walk to the back. I can tell that she's saying something to him but can't tell what it is.

Rosie says, "Don't get depressed. You know that's the way divorce parents get sometimes. I've been living with it for years. You'll get used to it."

"I hope so."

"You will. I promise." She watches as I put the boots back in the box. "Phoebe, you know all those novels about divorce? They're mostly for the kids who are just starting it. There should be one about a kid who's lived with it for a long time. Then you'd see that we all survive it."

Jim and Mindy return.

I don't know what she said to him, but he's in a much better mood.

Placing the pie in front of us, he says, "There it is— Woodstock Pizzeria's famous whole wheat pizza, with half extra cheese and the other half sausage. You know which part I want."

"The whole half." I pretend to faint.

He pretends to revive me. "No—just no sausage. Honey, your boots are very pretty. Tomorrow let's go to Woodstock Design and get a pair of leg warmers to go with them."

Rosie and Mindy start to laugh at the same time.

As my father sits down he says, "Let us in on the joke."

Mindy wipes a dab of sauce off her chin. "That sounds so familiar. Sometimes I buy something for Rosie that she doesn't need or even want because her father's just bought her something."

"Anything you can do I can do better?" My father hands her a napkin. "It's ridiculous, isn't it. I thought I was over doing that."

Rosie and I look at each other.

"I kind of like it," Rosie says. "It's one of the advantages of being a divorce kid."

"Me too." I pick up a piece of pizza. The extra cheese slithers onto my hand. "How about a trip to Hawaii? Then Mom'll have to take me to Europe."

"So much about divorce revolves around money. But then so did marriage." Mindy takes a sip of my father's apple cider before she realizes that it's not her Coke.

Finally we stop talking about divorce and I ask Mindy how her book is going.

She frowns. "It's rough. I've got a writer's block, nothing's working. The only writing I've done lately is graffiti."

"Graffiti." Rosie shakes her head as she puts red pepper on her slice. "My mother writes on walls."

"You try to bring parents up right, and this is the way they act." I pretend to sound stern. "Mindy, do you write dirty things on the wall?"

My father says, "I could always do the illustrations to go with the writing."

I shake my head. "She probably writes them on ladies' room walls. We'd have to get you into a disguise."

"A long blond wig," Rosie suggests.

"What do you write?" my father asks, starting to put salt on his pizza and then remembering he doesn't use it anymore.

Mindy picks up the salt and puts some on her slice. "My grandfather, who spoke very little English, had a favorite expression for all occasions. Writing it down is a way of keeping his memory alive."

"I have a feeling that I've seen it," I say.

She fills my father in. "I write 'Hoo ha—six o'clock.'"

We end up talking about all the stuff that we do that could get us into trouble. I tell the Krazy Glue story. Rosie tells about the time she had to stand in front of the room with gum on her nose as punishment for blowing a bubble in a class where the teacher did not allow gum. That reminds my father of the teacher who said, "Brooks, I want the gum in the garbage can in three minutes or you'll have detention." My father said, "But the flavor's not gone. What if I stand in the can—I can still chew it and the gum will be in the garbage." He never expected the teacher to say yes, but she did.

Finally my father says, "I hate to break up one of the best times I've had for a while, but there's homework to be done, and the kids have to get up at the crack of dawn."

"Hoo ha—six o'clock," I say as we leave.

10

Joyce Kilmer High School—it's so different from my school in New York. There are some things that are alike, but not many.

It's so big, from seventh grade up, in one building. That's like my old school, but here there are about three thousand kids. I'm used to about five hundred, from kindergarten up.

My old school was in a small brownstone building. Kilmer looks like it was once a giant car factory, only here they turn out students instead of cars.

My old school didn't even have a song. Here they sing one based on a poem by Joyce Kilmer, "Trees." I hate it.

About the kids—most of them are okay, but a few, who act as if they have a screw loose, should probably be recalled. There are about six towns that the kids come from, so there are eleven different types, like at most schools. There are the jocks, the brains, the skidders (who hang out in Woodstock, kind of hoods —the name comes from Skid Row, and there was once even a sign in some store that said NO SKIDDERS ALLOWED), the in crowd, the social outcasts (who don't have a friend to their names), and the regulars.

I guess I'm a regular, who some people think is a brain. I'm not sure I like being put in any group, but it's certainly better than being a social outcast.

I'm sitting in a boring math class, trying to figure out what the letters in my name spell when rearranged. Phoebe Anna Brooks. It's so hard. Finally I get one— Phone breaks a boon. That explains why I like to make telephone calls in between doing different homework assignments.

The bell rings.

Rush to lunch to get in line.

Try to get in front. The few edible things go fast, like cottage cheese and fruit, which they haven't yet figured out how to ruin.

Today's lunch is chicken a la king. Yesterday's was chicken croquettes. The day before that was chicken. I bet tomorrow we'll have spaghetti with chicken sauce. Puke. I'd bring my lunch, but nobody does, except for Alfie Fitch and he's a social outcast who totes his in a Strawberry Shortcake lunch box.

After paying for a meal that they should pay me to eat, I join Rosie and the other kids.

There's only one seat left, and it's at the end of the table next to Dave. He's in some of my classes—

smart, funny, and very cute. Once I asked Rosie about him, and she said he used to go out with her friend, the one who had to move away because of the custody decision. "Now," she said, "he's up for grabs. Lots of girls would love to go out with him but he doesn't seem interested."

Even though it doesn't show, I'm a little shy and nervous when I like a guy in the beginning. I just try to act as if I'm not.

I set my tray on the table and sit down, acting very calm.

Calm, ha! I'm so calm, I forget that I've got my knapsack on my arm. I've just hit Dave in the head with it. I can tell he's noticed, since he looks like he's trying to cover up pain.

"I'm so sorry. Would it make it any better if I just died right here and now of embarrassment?" I whisper.

He touches the left side of his head. "You don't have to do anything that extreme. However, you've just knocked out all the stuff I've ever learned by hitting me on the left side of the brain."

That's what we just studied in science, how the brain works.

"I'll be glad to tutor it all back into your brain again." I go along with his kidding. "However, a lot of what we learn in school isn't worth remembering."

"When I was little and got hurt, my mother always kissed the part that hurt." Dave looks at me.

"I'm glad I didn't drop the knapsack on your feet." I open up my milk container.

"I think my memory is returning. A miracle. I'm going to remember that you owe me a kiss," Dave says.

There are worse things, I think, and look down at my tray.

Rosie's complaining. "This food's awful."

"So what's new?" Pete holds up a piece of wilted lettuce.

"But it's getting worse," a girl named Jill says, and shakes her curly head. "Ever since the new company got the contract, it's to vomit over."

Sarah, who's in my English class and is very serious about becoming a ballerina, is getting ready to eat her creamed corn. "Do you mind? I'm trying to eat lunch."

"It looks like somebody's already vomited over it." Alex takes off his glasses and pretends to use them as a magnifying glass.

Sarah puts her fork down and pushes the tray away.

We all look at the food. Nobody's eating except Milton Myers, and I hear that even his own mother calls him Garbage Gut.

"I think we ought to do something about this." Dave bangs his fist on the table. "We've tried to talk to the administration, but they don't care."

Garbage Gut asks Sarah for her creamed corn. She passes it to him. Everyone else at the table gives theirs to him too.

He burps.

"Gross," Sarah says.

"Thank you." Garbage Gut takes another spoonful of corn.

Sometimes I don't understand how people get into groups. Garbage Gut's a perfect example of someone who should be a social outcast but isn't, and I bet there are lots of nice people who shouldn't be social outcasts but are.

I listen to the complaints and debate whether to get involved. After all, when I got here, the Principal called me in and said, "Phoebe Brooks, your record precedes you. I want no trouble. If I so much as see you with a tube of Krazy Glue in your hands, you'll be suspended."

Possession with the intent to use. Suspension. It sounds like a drug charge. I promised to be good. But the food is awful and school is so boring.

Finally I decide. "Listen, we had this problem at my old school, and there were certain things we did—and they worked."

Everyone's staring at me.

"Well, don't keep us in suspense. Tell us," Rosie says.

Dave has his elbow on the table and his chin on his hand, and he's staring at me.

I have a feeling that this is one time I should keep my big mouth shut.

"Well, it's this way . . ." I begin.

11

It's all set up. There's a meeting today, and I can go even though it's Saturday and I'm supposed to be in New York.

It wasn't easy getting my mother to agree. At first she asked if I didn't want to come in because of the thing about Katie and Andy. I told her no. Then she wanted to know if I still loved her. I told her yes. She reminded me that if I didn't go this time, we wouldn't see each other for a total of three weeks, since she has to work out of town next weekend. Finally she gave in when I promised that we'd have a really great Thanksgiving together.

It kind of bothered me when she said, as long as I wasn't coming in, she'd go out to the Hamptons with Duane, to call her there if I needed her. The Hamptons—Duane's got a beach house out there. It's all so fashionable and rich, and I can't stand it because the one time the three of us went, my mother and Duane slept in the same bedroom. After that I told her I didn't ever want to go again.

Now we have an arrangement. When I stay overnight, Duane doesn't. What they do when I'm not there I don't want to know about.

Maybe I'm a prude, but I don't like to think about my parents having sex with anyone but each other. Even that is more than I want to think about.

I pull on the lavender unicorn-shirt, jeans, cowboy boots, leg warmers. It sure is beginning to get cold here. I put a feather barrette in my hair.

All I need now is the ride to Rosie's.

My father calls out, "Phoebe, ready yet? I want to get to the sales early."

Garage sales. He's been doing a lot of them lately. Since he gave up work, he worries a lot about money and is trying to be careful, so that his savings last until he gets accepted into an art gallery. We used to have lots of money. I think my mother still does. My father, though, worries more and more about it lately. So do I.

"Ready, honey?" He picks up the car keys. "You look great."

I put on my sweat-shirt jacket.

"It's getting cold." He sighs. "You've grown a lot. We'll have to buy you a new coat."

"I'll get one when I see Mom," I say, and then, not wanting him to feel bad about the money, I add, "Or I can hold out till the January sales."

He shakes his head. "Don't be silly. We're not that poor."

"You pay for all the day-to-day stuff," I say, kissing him. "She can pay for the coat. After all, if I were living with her, she'd be paying more. In lots of families people pay child support to the parent who's got the kid most of the time. So don't worry."

As we get into the car he says, "If people had told me a few years ago that we'd be having this discussion, I'd have said they were nuts."

We drive in silence for a while.

If only I can think of a way to get him out of this mood.

"Guess what, Dad," I say. "When I went to Rosie's after school yesterday, she made us grilled cheese sandwiches."

"That's nice." He uses the voice that parents have when they really aren't interested.

I continue anyway. "She said that she didn't want to dirty the grill, so she took two slices of bread, some cheese, made a sandwich, and wrapped it in aluminum foil."

"That's nice," he repeats.

I start to giggle. "Then she took out an iron and ironed it."

He laughs and glances my way. "You're kidding."

"No, it's true and it works."

He says, "I guess that's one way to handle a pressing problem."

I groan and say, "We'll just have to remember that technique when things get all wrinkled up."

It makes me feel good when I can get him out of a bad mood.

12

Rosie's house is on Meade Mountain Road. Actually it's a carriage house, part of a much bigger property. The landlord lives in the big house and rents out what was once the place where servants lived.

It's not big, just cozy and right for two people, a cat, and a dog. Mindy and Rosie furnished most of the house with things from yard, house, garage, and estate sales. In New York City the stuff would probably be called antiques. Here it's called stuff.

I walk into the house, through the front porch. Mindy's got her typewriter and paper on the table. It's a mess, what she calls "creative disorder."

Rosie's at the kitchen sink, doing dishes. "Be with you in a minute."

I stoop down to pet Salamander, the dog.

He licks my face.

If only my father weren't allergic to animals.

Salamander's rolling over, wanting to be scratched.

As I scratch his stomach I feel something patting at my face.

It's Fig Newton, the cat. He's after my feather barrette.

I don't know what to do. If I move fast, he may decide to pounce. If I don't move, he may decide to pounce. What if he claws my hair or face?

"Rosie," I say, softly.

Rosie turns to me, sizes up the situation, and puts down the plate she is drying.

As she approaches, Fig Newton continues to bat the feather around.

His paw is getting closer and closer to my face.

Rosie comes up behind him, scoops him up, and puts him outside.

"Thanks." I take a deep breath. "For a minute I thought I was a dead duck."

"That'll teach you to wear feathers with Fig Newton around. He probably thought you were a bird."

"That would have been fowl," I say.

"That pun is definitely a down." Rosie throws a dish towel at me. "DUCK."

Mindy walks in. "Rosie, I've got to get to work. . . . Oh, hi, Phoebe. Listen, would you kids be careful and not touch my stuff on the table? I'm in the middle of a chapter and don't have time to clean up."

"We can eat lunch on the porch," Rosie says.

"Or go on a picnic," I suggest.

"A great idea." Mindy grabs her coat. "I'd rather do that than have to wait on people . . . but duty calls. See you tonight."

As she rushes out of the house Rosie says, "Sometimes I think I'm the grown-up in this house. Look at the mess she left."

My mother would have a fit if I did something like that, left everything lying around. It's a good thing she's not Mindy's mother, although I don't think she could be, since they're about the same age.

Rosie says, "The picnic sounds like fun. The meeting's not until two o'clock. Why don't we pack up some food and go walking by the stream?"

We make up some sandwiches and start the walk into town.

It's a beautiful Indian summer day. The trees are still colorful. The air is so clean, not at all like city air.

We walk down Meade Mountain Road, onto Rock City Road.

There are no sidewalks, so we've got to be careful of the passing cars.

Neither of us say much as we walk. Friends can be quiet together.

At Andy Lee Field there's a baseball game going on.

Past the cemetery. Someday I want to go in there and look at all the old tombstones, but it makes me a little nervous to think about dying.

Finally we end up right in the center of town.

Stopping to get a drink of water from the fountain

at the Village Green, I look at all of the people who are shopping, hanging out, eating ice cream cones.

"Let's go into Tinker Street Toys," I say, "and play."

We walk over to the store and go inside.

There's a table set up in the middle of the store with all sorts of windup toys.

Rosie and I have a race with two pairs of walking feet.

Her feet win.

My feet get all tangled up with a walking coffeepot that some little kid was playing with.

I decide to buy a bottle of bubble liquid.

As we leave the store I start to blow bubbles.

It looks great, all of the bubbles streaming down Tinker Street as if they are in a parade.

People are smiling at them.

Rosie and I walk over to Millstream Road and start walking on the edge of the stream.

Finally we stop and sit down on a dry rock. It's so still that I can hear the wind and the water moving.

After a few minutes Rosie breaks the silence. "My father called this morning and told my mother that the child support check was going to be late again this month. Mindy was really angry."

"What did she say?" I pick up a pebble and throw it in the stream.

"Most of what she said was profanity. She was really steamed up. He's such a creep sometimes. He just bought a whole bunch of electronic equipment. I don't see why he couldn't send the money. Sometimes I think he does it just to get her mad. You're so lucky that your parents don't do stuff like that."

I remember that when everything got split up, there was fighting. Maybe it's good there is no child support money to worry about. I'd feel responsible, even though I'd know it wasn't my fault.

Rosie opens her lunch. "It makes me feel cruddy, like he doesn't care about me. He spends all the money on his wife's two kids. . . . Sometimes he doesn't send the money, but he'll buy me a big present. Then it makes me feel disloyal to Mindy because I don't want to tell her about it."

"Do you need some money? My father's going to give me my allowance tomorrow. It's not much, but I'll share it."

"Thanks, pal." She reaches over and pats me on the head and then pulls at my feather barrette. "No. We're doing okay. Mindy's getting lots of tourist tips and I'm baby-sitting, so it's okay. It's not the money as much as it is the hurt. I don't know why my own father should act that way."

I tell her about how I feel, knowing that my mother's spending the weekend with Duane the Drip. How he always talks down to me as if I'm three years old and how he always acts as if he's so wonderful because he's so rich. I also let her know how uncomfortable I feel about their sleeping together.

"I know," Rosie says. "A couple of years ago this guy Ben moved in with us. That took a lot of getting used to."

"What happened?" I start eating my lunch.

"It just didn't work out. I was sorry when he left. I got used to the three of us being a family, and then he was gone. While he lived in Woodstock, I still saw him but then he moved away. He's in Florida now. I just got a letter from him. He's married and they just had a kid."

"Did he and Mindy fight a lot?" I think of my parents during their bad time.

"No. He wanted to marry Mindy. She wanted to leave things the way they were. So he left."

"Why didn't Mindy marry him? Doesn't she want to get married again?" I put a grape in my mouth.

"She's not sure . . . said it would have to be someone really special, that the first marriage was such a disaster that she was afraid of her own judgment. My father felt that way too. He waited a long time to get remarried." Rosie shakes her head.

"Do you ever want to get married?" I bite into my sandwich.

Rosie shrugs. "Who knows? I'm having enough trouble finding a boyfriend."

I look at two people who are walking in the middle of the stream with their pants legs rolled up. They are carrying their shoes and holding hands.

"You shouldn't have any trouble finding someone. Look at all the guys who are your friends."

She says, "Yeah, but none of them want to start dating yet. Why do girls have to grow up faster than boys? The guys who date want to go further than I do. Oh, well . . . I guess I'll just have to wait. Until someone comes along, I'll just baby-sit a lot so that it isn't a total loss."

We look at the water. There are lots of leaves in it, going downstream.

Rosie says, "So what about you?"

"I don't know. I kind of like Dave, a lot. I like him much more than I liked Andy." I blush. It's not easy to talk about something that I'm not sure is going to work out.

"He's nice, isn't he." Rosie pulls out an apple and bites down on it. "I think he likes you too."

I think for a minute. "I guess I want him to like me and be my boyfriend. But that's just for now. I don't know about later. If I'll ever get married or anything . . . Marriage just doesn't seem to work out for anybody."

"I know some that work," Rosie says. "Dave's parents are still together, and I think they're happy."

"But a lot don't. I guess I'll just have to wait and see."

"Why don't we go to the same college and be roommates and then when we graduate, we can get an apartment in New York and have careers?" Rosie says. "And if we ever do get married and have kids, we can be bridesmaids for each other and aunts to the kids."

"If I could choose a sister, it would be you." I close my lunch bag. "Somehow I never thought you'd be so traditional about weddings and stuff."

She picks up my bubble stuff and starts to play with it. "Maybe because Mindy is so untraditional. Don't kids have to do stuff to rebel against their parents? Maybe the only way I can go against her is to be real straight."

I laugh. "You can get all dressed up each day in three-piece suits and be real conservative."

She shakes her head. "I don't think that's going to happen, but I've never really been part of a whole happy family or even an unhappy family. My parents split up when I was a baby. I'd like to have a good family."

"I promise to be your bridesmaid and baby-sit for your kids if that does happen."

"Okay, now let's figure out what our apartment's going to look like," she says.

We sit by the stream and make plans for what our lives are going to be like when we're on our own. Rosie's much more sure of what it's going to be like. She's obviously thought about it a lot. I haven't. I think much more about the present. She thinks more about the future.

The only future I'm really thinking about right now is whether or not I'm going to see Dave at the meeting.

13

The first meeting of KRAPS is about to take place.

KRAPS stands for Kilmerites Rebel Against Poor Sustenance. Personally I think the group name is a little obnoxious, but I was outvoted.

Rosie and I ring the doorbell. Sarah Bennett answers it. "Everyone's in the living room. Go in. I'll be there in a minute."

Rosie leads the way because she's been here before and I haven't.

The house is absolutely beautiful, all natural wood and all the furniture in earth colors. It's large, with high ceilings.

Everyone's sitting by the fireplace. Some are on chairs, a lot are on cushions.

Dave's not here yet. There are about twenty kids

already present and there should be about thirty, so maybe he'll arrive soon.

Sarah brings out dip and vegetables. There is already some great-looking food on the table—apple slices with melted cheese, granola cookies, carob candies.

Garbage Gut downs a couple of carob candies.

Jennifer Farley says, "Milt, how come you're here? You like the school food."

He doesn't answer until she asks him the same question, calling him Garbage Gut.

I can't believe it. He seems to prefer that awful nickname because he stops eating long enough to answer. "My father, the dentist, said that I should come here. Anyway, I like parties."

His father, the dentist. . . . I think about Rosie's comment about kids having to rebel. It's a good thing that Garbage Gut's father isn't a policeman.

The kids are all sitting around talking.

Wendy Aaronson pulls out a cigarette and lights up.

Sarah walks up to her. "Listen, if you want to smoke, you're going to have to do it outside. We don't let anyone smoke in the house. The smell . . . plus we care too much about people to be part of their harming themselves."

Wendy says "Okay" and goes out the side door.

"That was done nicely," I say.

Sarah nods. "My parents used to smoke, and then my uncle died of lung cancer."

More kids arrive. Some are from Woodstock. Others are from other towns. That's good because sometimes only the Woodstock kids get involved in causes, like leftover hippies from the sixties. Also, it's hard for all the kids to get together because there's no public transportation.

Abby Streetman. Harry Marcus. The school couple. They go everywhere with their arms around each other. Most of the time his hand is in her back jeans pocket. Sometimes I wonder if it has to be surgically removed every time they go to class or home.

Pete Redding. The school clown. He does the best imitation of teachers and the Principal.

Holly Marham. Willow Smith. Meredith Cooper. The three of them are always together unless two of them decide to gang up on the third. That usually lasts for only a few days and then they are all back together until the next fight.

Still no Dave.

Oh, well, I've got to remember that the real reason for being here is to work on the committee.

The work begins.

Everyone starts talking about the steps already taken . . . letters sent to the Principal and the school board . . . trying to talk to the Principal and nutritionist. Nothing has worked.

I take a piece of broccoli and stick it in the dip.

It's interesting to watch everyone. Even though there's some joking, everyone's serious about the subject, except for Garbage Gut, who keeps saying things like "I love hot dogs. . . . What's wrong with processed cheese? . . . So what if potato chips have a little grease?"

"Any suggestions besides the things that Phoebe told us they did at her old school?" Rosie picks up a notebook and pen.

"Why don't we have a commando raid on the kitchen, take it over, and make our own meals?" Sarah practices a ballet step as she talks.

"Illegal," Rosie says. "We want to stay within the law."

"I thought of a new one." I raise my hand, forgetting that we're not in school. "I guess by now that most of you know I have this weird habit of rearranging letters in words so that they mean other things."

"Those are called anagrams," Steve Gleason says, pushing his glasses back.

"An A-plus for the Poindexter." Pete waves a piece of cauliflower.

Rosie shakes her head. "Yeah, you rearranged my name, and I ended up with I SORE. What a friend."

Abby stops making out with Harry long enough to call out, "See what our two names are when they are put together."

"Your two names together are going to spell out BABY if you aren't careful." Garbage Gut cradles his arms as if he's got an infant in them.

Harry makes an obscene gesture to Garbage Gut. Then he and Abby go back to making out.

"Continue." Rosie nods to me, trying to get back to the subject.

"Well, I tried it with CAFETERIA and ended up with several things." Taking out my list, I read from it. "Here are some . . . I TEAR FACE . . . EAT FAR ICE . . . AFTER I, ACE."

"That would be good to use when someone cuts in

front of the cafeteria line," Sarah calls out, using a chair to practice leg extensions.

"Better than flat tires, even," Jill says, braiding Wendy's hair.

Garbage Gut does flat tires a lot. That's when someone behind you steps on the back of your shoes and the shoes come off.

I continue to read from the list. "I CEE A RAFT . . . I.E. FAT RACE . . . I.E. RAT FACE . . . FACE IT, EAR . . . I CARE, FEAT. . . ."

"Not bad." Pete Redding does his imitation of Mr. Morley, the math teacher. "But could you get to the point? Remember the shortest distance between two points is a straight line, Ms. Brooks. You're taking the long cut."

"Okay. Listen to this one . . . CITE A FEAR. That's it. We can write that on a piece of paper and everyone can tell what their worst fear is about the cafeteria."

"I like it," Willow Smith says.

Holly and Meredith agree. So do the other kids.

Dave walks in the door. He's out of breath. His blond hair is flopping in front of his brown eyes.

I'd love to go over to him and brush the hair off his face but decide that would be a bit much.

He walks through the crowd and sits down next to me. "Sorry I'm late. I had to do some errands before I could get the car to come over here."

Rosie looks at me and smiles.

Jill says, "I've made up a list of committees to work on. Everyone sign up and get to work."

As people get up to look at the paper, Dave turns to me. "I have an idea too. I stopped at the library to get a copy of 'Trees.' "

"I figure you should know it by heart, since we have to sing it in assemblies all the time."

"No one pays attention to the stuff they make you memorize in school. . . . Look, let's work together on it."

"Okay. So what's the idea?" I really want to brush the hair out of his eyes.

"You know how English teachers are always telling us that parodies make fun of an established work. Well, I think we should do one of 'Trees'—and then we can get the whole school to sing it at an assembly when we're supposed to do the school song."

"I love it," I say. "Let's get to work."

We pick up two pillows and go sit in a corner. Kids all over the room are working. Even though there's a lot of joking, everyone's serious, except maybe Garbage Gut. It's interesting. In Woodstock a lot of grown-ups are active politically—fighting for good causes, like against nuclear plants, getting rid of the gypsy moths without using dangerous sprays, people's rights. There's even a runaway house and a battered women's shelter. I think that when kids grow up seeing their parents involved, the kids get involved too.

Dave and I look at the poem. It feels comfortable being with him.

We start to laugh as we begin the parody. A couple of kids come over to see what's so funny. When they realize what we're doing, everyone joins in.

When it's finished, Pete does his imitation of Ms. Douglass, the English teacher. He pretends to readjust a bra strap, points into the air, and says, "Well, class. . . . It's not Shakespeare, but at least it rhymes."

CAFETERIA
(*to be sung to* "Trees")

I think that I shall never see
A cafeteria as gross as thee.

A cafeteria where hungry mouths are pressed
Against food that's really messed

A cafeteria that looks at kids all day
Who have fears of ptomaine, so they say

A cafeteria that may each day wear
Out stomach linings that will tear.

Upon whose food lines people have lain
People crying and writhing while in pain

Poems are made by fools like me,
But a cafeteria like this drives me up a tree.

14

We're ready.

Someone's father's got a Xerox machine, and we've got all the copies of the song.

One person in each homeroom quietly distributes the paper.

There's a note attached.

IF YOU CARE ABOUT IMPROVING THE QUALITY OF CAFETERIA FOOD, SING THIS AT ASSEMBLY TODAY. IF YOU DON'T, JUST KEEP QUIET. NOBODY LIKES A SQUEALER.

We march into assembly, sitting down quietly. It's the kind of quiet where you know that something's going to happen.

The Principal announces the speaker, a member of the D.A.R., Daughters of the American Revolution.

Somehow that seems appropriate.

The Principal continues. "Now, let's all welcome her with a rousing rendition of our school song."

Rousing isn't quite the word for it.

I don't think the real song has ever been sung so clearly, so loudly, by so many people.

Probably the Principal, Mr. Beasley, doesn't want to create a scene about what's just happened, although he's got this weird look on his face, like he doesn't know whether to laugh or cry.

Some of the kids, and teachers too, do laugh. Even when the speaker is talking about how her ancestors took part in the American Revolution, every once in a while there's a little chuckle from someplace, and trust me, this lady's not doing a comedy routine.

The bell rings.

After applauding the boring speaker, we file out.

All day long everyone's expecting something to be said by Beasley. But nothing is. Amazing.

By the end of the day there's still no word.

I'm at my locker, getting ready to go home.

Dave shows up. Even though his locker's at the other end of the hall, he seems to be in this vicinity a lot.

"So what do you think they're going to do?" He holds my books as I put on my coat.

"I don't know." I take back the books. "I kind of expected something, like putting all of us in front of a firing squad, or detention, at least."

He says, "Well, on to Phase Two tomorrow."

"I know. They won't be able to ignore that."

We walk out to the bus.

Drat. He's not on my bus. I wish he were. But then I'd have to make a decision about who to sit with, Dave or Rosie.

Today I can't sit with either of them. Rosie's not going home on this bus. She's got detention for cracking her knuckles in Music Appreciation class. She was doing it in time to the *1812 Overture*. Some teachers have no sense of humor.

We stop in front of my bus.

"What's your middle name?" I ask. "Since I don't have much homework tonight, maybe I'll try to figure what it is rearranged."

"A-L-L-E-N." He brushes the hair out of his eyes. "How about letting me know what you come up with when we go out this Saturday night? . . . That is, if you want to go out."

Want to go out? Do I want a million dollars? Do I want the sky to fill with rainbows?

I calmly say, "I'd love to." Inside I feel like my body's got a Ping-Pong game going on.

"Okay, you kids. No playing Romeo and Juliet," the bus driver bellows. "This bus is going to leave on schedule."

"See you in school tomorrow," Dave says as he rushes off to catch his bus.

Rushing up the steps, I have to listen to the driver say, "You kids think the world waits for you." She points a finger at me. "Remember. Next time I'll leave you behind."

As the bus lurches forward I take the first available

seat I find. It's next to this kid in my gym class. Lark McKeon.

She looks up from her math homework. "Lucky. I'd give anything to have Dave Shore pay that much attention to me."

I look at her face to try to figure out if she's being nasty but decide that she means it.

Lark says, "Actually I do have a boyfriend, but he's in the Army. . . . Doesn't that bus driver just drive you nuts? Last year, my boyfriend, who was a senior, and I were two minutes late getting to the bus and she drove off without us. She saw us running and she left anyway. . . . Look, do you want to see a picture of him?"

Before I can even answer, she's got her wallet out and she's showing me pictures. Lark and Mark at the Prom . . . at the Library Fair . . . Mark in uniform. She's the fastest talker in the world. I don't even have a chance to say anything.

Finally she puts her wallet away. "Actually I started going out with him because I like the way our names sound together. Lark and Mark. But then I really started liking him. I miss him. I miss having a boy-friend here. It gets boring without one. Actually it's pretty boring even with one."

Actually I'm beginning to think that Lark's pretty boring. . . . No wonder her life isn't exciting. She's got to listen to herself talk all day.

I stare at her forehead, right between the eyes. It's something I've learned to do when I'm supposed to look interested. It comes in handy in school and other places.

The bus pulls up at her stop.

As she stands up to leave she says, "We'll have to talk more often. That was fun. When Mark comes home on leave, maybe we can double."

"But Dave and I aren't a couple." I manage to get in a word, several in fact.

"Good. That's settled. I'll tell Mark when I write to him tonight."

She's gone.

Some girls turn into absolute fluffbrains when they go out with a guy. Something tells me that Lark started out that way though.

The bus pulls up at my stop and I get out.

"Don't forget what I said," the bus driver yells.

I pretend not to hear her.

My father's out by the pool, painting the view of the reservoir.

There are leaves all over the pool cover.

Winter is definitely on its way.

I stand on the patio and look down at him. "Want to take a break?"

He looks up. There's a smudge of paint on his cheek. "Oh, hi, honey. No thanks. I want to keep working as long as there's light."

"Okay, see you later." I go into the house.

I really wanted to tell him about my date with Dave . . . and what happened in school with the assembly. Sometimes I get jealous of the time he spends painting, and then I think that's better than his being with some woman I wouldn't like.

Going into the refrigerator for juice, I see that he's made dinner for tonight. Salad. A cheese casserole.

I'll prepare a special dinner for him on the night I go out with Dave so that he doesn't feel lonely.

Before I start my homework, I take out my notebook and tear out little scraps of paper and put a letter on each one.

D A V I D A L L E N S H O R E

It takes forever to come up with a good combination.

Finally I come up with something. . . . It sounds like one of those awful romance novels.

Wait till I tell Rosie. . . . HIS DEAR LOVE LAND and PHONE BREAKS A BOON are going out.

15

Phase Two—Double B-Day.

B&B—Bread and Butter.

Everyone goes through the line, buying one slice of bread and two pats of butter.

The bread gets buttered, with more butter around the edges.

A few minutes before the bell is to ring, Jill goes up to the cafeteria teachers, who are all standing in one place, probably discussing how they got stuck with such a lousy assignment.

Jill asks for a bathroom pass.

That's the signal.

Everyone quietly sticks the bread to the underside of the table top, butter side up.

The teachers tell Jill to wait until the bell rings, since

the period's almost over. They always say that to
kids. They think that kidneys can tell time.

The bell rings.

Everyone rushes out of the place. I don't think the
cafeteria's ever been emptied out so quickly.

Later we get the report from the kids who have
lunch next.

The bread falls down—piece by piece.

Cafeteria workers freak out.

The janitors rush around cleaning it up while kids
are trying to get lunch and be seated.

No bread and butter is served for this group.

We figured that would happen. So everyone buys
the yucky yellow cake with the awful yellow icing
and mushes it under the table.

This time Beasley does react.

I'm in Algebra class figuring out that the letters in
the word ALGEBRA spell out REAL GAB when
Beasley gets on the intercom.

"All senior high students are to report to the school
auditorium immediately."

Mr. Michaels, our teacher, says, "Okay, everyone
line up."

"What about me?" Eric Parker, child genius, raises
his hand.

Eric's only nine, but the grammar school has him
in high school academic courses. He's so smart, they
don't know what to do with him. However, he's not
real bright about asking. He should have just gone.
That's the problem with child geniuses. Academically
they do fine. It's socially that's a problem.

Michaels shrugs. "Why don't you go back to your old school and have recess?"

Michaels hasn't liked Eric since the day Eric corrected one of Michaels's mistakes.

"The assembly may not be acceptable for you." Michaels puts books in his briefcase. "We have to go."

What's he expecting, an R-rated assembly?

Eric says, "Okay, give me a pass to the library. I'll do some work on the computer."

"Good idea," Michaels says.

Good for Eric. He didn't let Michaels's remark get to him. And I've seen him work on the computer before. He's got Space Invaders programmed on it.

We march down to the auditorium. Some kids look nervous. Others smile a lot.

Beasley is on the auditorium stage pacing as everyone sits down.

This time he does react.

He starts to speak.

Something tells me that this time no one is going to get the chance to sing "Trees."

He grips the podium. "What's going on?"

The room is quiet. The only sound is the auditorium clock ticking.

Dave raises his hand. We've decided that he should be spokesperson.

Beasley calls on him.

"We've all complained about the cafeteria food before, and no one has done anything about it. We just wanted to emphasize our dissatisfaction."

Dave's speaking very calmly. I'm proud of him. I'm

so glad he's asked me out. I'm glad he called me last night. At Kilmer that's how people "go out," by making phone calls and walking around the halls together. When you're a kid, it's hard to have lots of real dates. One good thing is that he's older and has his license, so we'll have a chance to spend some time together. I hope that he's a good kisser. I definitely like good kissers.

Dave continues. "Civil disobedience is the cornerstone of a democracy. We just wanted to be democratic about it."

Beasley snorts. "Wouldn't it have been easier to send a telegram? Did you have to disrupt a school assembly, embarrass a guest, and ruin school property?"

Dave speaks firmly. "No property was ruined. We realize that there was a mess to deal with, but there was no willful destruction."

Beasley doesn't listen. He talks about the Kilmer school spirit and how we should stand behind the school, no matter what.

Maybe we *should* send him a telegram. That's expensive, but if we can keep it under ten words, it shouldn't be too bad.

> ROSES'RE RED,
> VIOLETS BLUE.
> THE FOOD STINKS.
> SO DO YOU.

Beasley keeps talking. "I don't like the food any better than you do. What do you think? That the administration and staff have their lunches catered? We have to eat the same food as you do."

Teachers get to cut in line and they get the few good things first. In the morning they can also put things aside for later. And one day I saw my home-room teacher send a note down to the cafeteria staff asking for special food.

I tried asking a cafeteria worker to please put aside a cottage cheese and fruit platter for me.

She said, "What do you think this is? The Culinary Institute?"

So it's not the same.

It's like the book that we're reading in English, *Animal Farm*, by George Orwell.

Some animals are more equal than others. (Especially if they're teachers.)

Beasley ends up by saying that the foolishness has to stop, that no one will be punished if everything goes back to normal.

We all troop out of assembly.

On to Phase Three.

16

"Phoebe, do you really think you need four sandwiches, twenty granola cookies, an apple, and two pears for one lunch?" my father asks.

I nod. "It's for Garbage Gut. I can't believe he's so skinny with all that he eats. If I ate half of what he does, I'd have to be rolled around." I pack another lunch.

My father pulls out a new batch of granola cookies from the oven. "I've got to hand it to you," he says. "You kids are really organized."

We are. Phase Three is: Everyone brings lunch. No one buys it. That's why my father and I are doing this—to help out the kids who can't make their own lunch, for one reason or another.

Garbage Gut said he'd bring his own, but we were

afraid that he'd still be hungry and not be able to keep away from the cafeteria line.

My assignment is to bring five extra lunches. At first I was kind of worried about whether doing this would put us over our food budget, but my father says not to worry.

As I put a new batch of cookies into the oven, I think maybe I am turning into a worrywart about money. I've never thought about it so much, but when my parents were married they never used to talk about it either.

I guess I'm thinking a lot about it today because my father's mother called. Grandmother Brooks is still absolutely freaked out that he's quit his job. She says things to me like, "Put your father, the bum, on the phone" and "I hope that he doesn't think he can come to me for money when he runs out."

I really do hate her. She's never been nice to him. He's never gone to her for money. I know he's not going to start now.

It did scare me a little, though, and I know he was upset when he got off the phone after talking to her.

He's okay now. After the call, he went out and worked on his painting. It's so beautiful . . . filled with nature and bright colors. I think he's doing the right thing.

If only he gets accepted to a gallery, everything will be fine. It is kind of strange, though, living in this really nice house with a swimming pool and worrying about money. It's a weird kind of poor.

"The new painting really looks good." I continue to work on the lunches.

"Bob Miller saw the painting, likes it, and wants it for the new house he's building."

"Oh, Dad. That's fantastic." I stop taking cookies off a sheet and hug him.

He whirls me around the kitchen. "It is wonderful. And—guess what? We're using the barter system. He's getting the painting and we're getting three cords of wood and he'll help install our new wood stove."

Wood stoves save on heating bills. In the City, heat always comes up like magic in radiators and the landlord is responsible. In Woodstock, people try to keep the oil costs down by using wood. I wish we didn't have the wood stove, since it's installed right in the fireplace. It's not so pretty.

Sometimes I feel like a pioneer. When you live in New York City, you never think about raccoons eating your garbage, or pipes freezing up, or trading for firewood. You do think about stuff like garbage strikes (I always think that phrase sounds funny. Can you imagine a bunch of garbage looking at each other and saying, "Hey, man, let's go out on strike"?) You also think about getting mugged. I know lots of kids there who carry extra money so that if they get mugged, the muggers don't hit them for not having enough. There are lots of good things about New York City, so I don't want people to get the wrong impression. Plays, music, museums, more kinds of people and experiences. I'm lucky to have both places.

The phone rings.

My father picks it up.

It's my mother. I can tell by the way he talks to her, kind of friendly but a little guarded. It's changed over the years. At first it was kind of awful. Then it was kind of a false getting-along. Now it's pretty good. I guess that parents go through stages when they split up.

Mine sure did—the fighting and anger—then the distance—and making me feel caught in the middle. After the divorce they try to be "civilized." I know that there were even times that they missed each other. I know for a fact that after the divorce they even slept with each other once in a while. It was confusing. Now they act like people who have a past history together, but only a future of knowing each other because of me.

He motions to me. "It's your mother. Why don't you take this upstairs?"

I run up the steps and pick up the phone to hear her saying "Yes. Things are going wonderfully. Traveling's great. Money's not bad. It's very exciting."

"I'm on," I let them know.

My father hangs up.

At first my mother and I talk about general stuff, like how school and work are going and how we miss each other.

Finally she lets me know what's really happening. With a sigh she says, "I just wanted to call. I miss you so much. Sometimes I feel so lonely. I feel like I'm not a real part of your life anymore."

I try to convince her that's not true, but I do know that it is different because I don't see her every day.

Then she tells me that she and Duane have broken up.

I debate saying "No loss" but keep quiet.

Now she's crying. It's over. She's sad. She's lonely.

She wishes I were there to keep her company. She's sorry that she's laying all of this on me, but she needs someone to talk to.

It's almost as if my mother's forgotten that I'm the daughter and she's the mother.

I tell her that it's going·to be all right, that she'll meet someone else, someone better . . . or do fine by herself.

Finally she says, "I guess this isn't fair to do to you. I just miss you. Three weeks apart is a long time, and this year is the first time in sixteen years that I've lived alone this much."

What to say is a problem. I love her and want to make things all better for her but why can't I just be a kid, one who has parents with problems they can handle by themselves? Or even better would be parents without problems.

After we finish talking, I go back downstairs.

"How's your mother?" my father asks.

"Fine," I say.

FAMILY. Rearrange the letters and it spells MY FAIL. I'm not sure that I know any families that really get along, except Dave's and the Parsons and they moved to Minnesota.

I wonder how Rocky and her family are doing. Do raccoons ever divorce? If so, who gets custody of the kids?

Oh, well—I can't control my parents' ups and downs. It's hard enough to cope with my own.

I think about Phase Three and wonder if it's going to work.

I'll find out soon.

17

CITE A FEAR

Our Teeth Rot(a)
Our Bodies languish(b)
Food cold and hot(a)
Causes Our Bodies anguish(a)

b?

⓸ The Cafeteria staff doesn't
Wash their hands after
going to the toilet.

~~signed~~

An English Student
Studing Rhyme Scheme

Lousy → Poem
D-

PEOPLE DROOL (ON THE FOOD)
GOING THRU LINE.

THE LEFTOVERS FROM BIO. LAB
ARE IN THE MYSTERY MEAT.

The Cafeteria Lady who picks
her nose drops some into
the Carrot & Raisin mixture.

The fruit
has been sprayed
with pesticides.

THE TAPIOCA GLASSES
HAVE BROKEN RIMS—
AND IT GETS INTO
THE FOOD.

I found worms in my food.
So I found slugs.
So I caught hepatitus

The Jello's cut in chunks
Because someone lost his
false teeth in the mold
and they had to cut through
to get it.

WARNING: The Surgeon General has Determined
That Cafeteria Eating Is Dangerous to your Health

That's as far as CITE A FEAR got. We put up a large piece of brown paper on the wall by the cafeteria entrance, and the kids started writing on it.

Beasley pulled it down. He also gave detention to one kid he caught writing on it, Pete. Pete wrote the terrible poem but he shouldn't have gotten detention. He got the rhyme scheme almost right.

Personally I think that Pete carried the protest a bit too far, lying down on the floor and yelling stuff like, "I regret that I have but one life to give for my stomach." "Don't shoot till you see the whites of their bread." And "Ask not what your food service can do for you—but what you can do for your food service."

Anyway now he's a martyr for the cause. He's got two days of detention and has to write a poem apologizing.

The boycott's working. Only about ten kids cross the cafeteria line.

We were going to have picket lines and carry signs but decided that we could get into trouble for that, and there was no need to do it.

Not buying food was enough. The cafeteria was stuck with about eighty billion hot dogs (you know the kind—they float them in water with little globs of grease) and beans (the pale orange ones with watered down sauce). Some of the stuff they could freeze, but a lot of it they couldn't.

It's really wasteful to throw it away with people starving in the world, but I'm sure they'd die of malnutrition from our cafeteria food anyway.

The cafeteria workers come out, look at all the kids eating homemade lunches, and shake their heads.

Beasley walks in, looks like he's going to say something but doesn't, and storms out.

We go on with our classes, but somehow cafeteria is what everyone focuses on, the kids at least.

Some teachers ignore the whole thing. Others like Mr. Cohen, the Civics teacher, use it to teach us history or literature. They talk about Henry David Thoreau, Gandhi, and Martin Luther King, Jr., all people who protested without use of violence.

The boycott goes on for three days.

My father and I continue to make extra lunches.

My mother calls every night, and I try to tell her what's going on, but she's kind of wrapped up in her own problems and just wants me to listen.

I try not to think about her too much and try to concentrate on the boycott. That's a lot easier to deal with.

It's fun. We all trade our lunches with each other. Some of the kids are bringing great food. I eat tofu, alfalfa sprouts, and mung bean salad. And a sandwich made of pickled herring and radishes. Never again will I eat a sandwich like that.

By the end of the third day Beasley makes an announcement over the loudspeaker.

"All students willing to work on a committee to change school menus are invited to a meeting next Tuesday night. Interested parents are also invited. Please plan to buy lunches again. We will do our best to serve food that meets your requests, within reason."

The cheering can be heard all over the school.

We won the battle, fair and square.

Nobody really even lost, because the food will be better for everyone.

18

Date Night with Dave—it sounds like some Cable TV show but it's not. It's my first chance to be alone with Dave.

I get dressed. Basic jeans and sweater.

I guess I should feel really uptight and nervous since this is Dave's and my first date, but I don't.

We've been walking to class and talking on the phone a lot.

Mostly I just feel happy that I'll be able to spend some time with him—without interruptions like some teacher saying, "Move along now—don't be late for class," or my father saying, "Phoebe, if you don't get off that phone soon, it's going to be permanently attached to your ear," and Godzilla the bus driver yelling.

I look in the mirror to check myself out. Brown hair to my shoulders, brown eyes, pale skin saved from total whiteness by a touch of blush-on—an okay but not great body. I don't think that anyone's going to ask me to pose for the cover of *Glamour*, but I don't think it's necessary to go out into the world covered by a yard-size Hefty garbage bag either.

I put on some jasmine oil and go into the living room.

My father's sitting down, reading the *Woodstock Times* and laughing at one of the funny Homecoming ads. Not only are the ads great, I love the store.

He looks up and says, "Phoebe, you look beautiful."

I go over and kiss him on the forehead. "You just say that because you're my father."

He shakes his head.

I look at him. He's not wearing paint-covered clothes. In addition to the handmade sweater he bought when he and Mom went to Scotland, he's got on a new pair of jeans. He looks pretty good for an older man.

The phone rings.

He shakes his head. "It's for you. It's always for you."

I get it.

It's Rosie. She's getting ready to baby-sit.

Rosie and I tell each other what we're wearing. Even though we both try to do things that don't conform, in some ways we are typical. What's the use of having a best friend if you don't tell each other what you're wearing and get the other person's reaction?

Rosie says softly, "My mother's really in a good mood tonight. I bet she's got a date with someone special. She hasn't been this up in a long time."

"Did you ask her?"

"She said it was private and smiled." Rosie continues. "You know—parents and their other lives."

I look at my father, who's still reading the paper, and wonder about what changes he makes when I don't go into the City over the weekend. I bet Mindy has to cope differently, too, when Rosie's father is on tour and she stays in Woodstock.

I don't think there's anyone serious in my father's life or he would have told me. We once made a deal that if there was ever anyone who might be in the running as future stepmom, he'd let me meet her and get used to the whole thing. That happened only once—when we were in New York—but it was soon after the divorce, and my father got involved too fast. I hated her. Alexandra. She used to call me "sweetie pie" and pretend she was crazy about me. But she wasn't. Kids know stuff like that. Anyway all she really wanted to do was get married. They knew I couldn't stand her. I don't know why he ever thought about marrying her. Maybe because he was just used to being married. Anyway he ended it. Phew. Close call.

The doorbell rings.

Dave.

I don't believe it. He's gotten his hair cut. Now

you can see his eyes. He still looks great, but I liked his hair longer.

Dave and my father shake hands.

They look each other up and down, trying not to let it show, and then my father "casually" starts asking questions.

"How are you? How old are you? Have you been driving long? What time do you expect to be home?"

I giggle. "Dad—Dave's a solid citizen, honor society, never a car accident."

"I used to be a Boy Scout. You know what good clean lives they live."

My father grins. "I hope that you got a merit badge for proper conduct on a date."

Dave grins right back at him. "Yes, sir. I also got one for not making fathers worry unnecessarily."

"Fine." My father nods.

I can tell that they like each other. Good. I don't mention that while Dave might have been a pillar of the Boy Scout community, I dropped out of Brownies before I even got into Girl Scouts. And the only badge I hope that Dave earned was in lifesaving—specializing in mouth-to-mouth resuscitation.

As we walk out the door my father yells after us. "Dave."

"Yes, sir."

"I was once a Boy Scout too. Watch it."

Finally we're out the door.

Dave and I look over at the reservoir. It's beautiful, clear, starry, a full moon.

It's also very cold. Winters in Woodstock are frigid

—it's only November and already I'm freezing, even with my new coat, boots, and leg warmers on. I'll probably thaw out in the spring.

I shiver, and Dave puts his arm around me. "We better get into the car."

I nod, shaking a little.

He guides me to the car and opens the door. "I know—you can do it yourself but not with your hands in your pockets."

I get in on my side.

He gets in on his, turns on the motor, and takes my hands in his to warm them up.

"Tiny hands," he says, putting his right hand flat against my left one.

"I know." My teeth are chattering a little. "I buy my gloves in the children's department."

He smiles and, still holding my hand, kisses me.

I kiss back.

We look at each other and smile.

"Dinner," he says. "How about The Little Bear?"

I love that place. Chinese food. I nod.

He puts the car into gear, and we drive up the road. It's easier now to see the houses that were hidden when the trees had leaves. Woodstock, changing seasons, is a magical place . . . familiar but new.

As we drive I say, "You got a haircut."

"I got a lot of hair cut." Dave frowns. "I know—bad joke . . . bad haircut. . . . My mother said if I wanted to borrow the car, I had to go to the barber. I can't wait till I save enough money to buy my own car. . . . Does it look awful?" He runs his hand over his forehead.

I shake my head. "No. I was just looking forward to pushing the hair out of your eyes."

"Pretend," he says.

I do, as he pulls into the parking lot of the restaurant.

As we park I see a car with a deer tied to it. Hunting season. It makes me sick.

It must show, because Dave says, "It bothers me too. Don't look."

He parks far from that car and we go into the place.

We walk up to the woman who is to seat us. The restaurant looks crowded, as always. I hope we don't have to wait too long.

"A table reserved for Shore," Dave says.

This kid's got class, I think.

Once we get seated at a table near the stream, I look out the window. It's the same stream that Rosie and I sat by, only it's much further down the road. I think about how happy I am.

We order ginger ale and look at the menus.

My parents and I used to come here a lot before the divorce, but my dad and I haven't been here lately.

I say, "This isn't cheap. We're definitely not at a fast-food place. Let's go dutch." Even though I'm not sure I've got enough money with me to pay.

He shakes his head. "Not this time. I raked a lot of leaves to pay for this. It's worth it."

"This meal could probably have paid something toward buying your car, a tire at least." I decide not to make him feel uncomfortable and say, "I know this menu. I want the chicken, veggies, garlic, and mushrooms. It's my favorite."

"Good. I'll order the shrimp and the appetizer assortment for two."

"Great. I love to share." I can feel my mouth start to water.

This is definitely not cafeteria food on the way.

As we eat he tells me more about his family. "It was the pits being the youngest. My older brother and sister always used to pick on me. When we visited my grandparents' farm, Doug named a stream after himself. Denise got the bridge."

"What about you?" I say, trying to coordinate my chopsticks around a dumpling.

"They named a puddle after me."

I laugh. "Not fair."

"It was seasonal. Besides, the puddle only filled up when it rained."

We both laugh.

He continues. "And once they were both remembering how our grandmother used to warn them to be careful when they walked in the field or an eagle would swoop down and get them."

"That must have really scared you," I say.

He shakes his head and smiles. "No one ever warned *me*. In fact, when I was older Doug said he'd taught me to say 'Here, birdie' and then sent me into the field. . . . We tease each other a lot but really do care."

"I miss a lot being an only child."

He nods. "There are good and bad things about having a brother and sister, but I mostly like it."

I think about how Rosie is the closest thing to having a sister, but it's not the same as being in the same house.

We both talk about a lot of stuff—growing up, what we like.

I like hearing that he's got a family that gets along so well. I hope that this one doesn't move to Minnesota too.

I really wish I weren't an only child. If there were another kid, we could share the responsibility of our parents.

By the time Dave and I eat our way to the fortune cookies, I'm talking to him about the thing that's bothering me the most. "Dave, you know I have to be in New York a lot of weekends . . . and over some vacations . . . and part of the summer."

He nods and frowns. "I know. I almost didn't ask you out because of that. I went through it with Cindy. But I like you a lot, so I guess we'll have to live with it."

"I like you a lot too. Darn parents. Why do they have to screw things up and then the kids have to do so much of the work?"

"But if they hadn't split up, then you would just have been one of the summer people I never would have met," he says, picking up his fortune cookie and breaking it open.

"What's your fortune?" I ask, wanting to change the subject.

He reads, "Boy who dates girl riding the Divorce Express will find happiness weekdays."

I grab the cookie.

It really says, "You will meet a tall dark stranger."

I open my cookie and read, "Girl who rides Divorce Express will look forward to Mondays."

He glances at my real fortune. "You will have many children."

I blush when he reads that but say, "I promise if I do to warn them about the eagles."

After he pays the check, we go back to the car and ride to Woodstock.

Trying to window-shop, we realize that it's too cold.

I hear music coming from the Joyous Lake, but we're too young to go there. It's a drag not to have places to go.

I wonder if my father's gone there but don't want to think about it.

When we get back to the house, my father's car is gone.

Dave comes in for a while.

We put on some music, pull up some cushions to sit on, and look out at the reservoir.

The full moon makes the whole area light up. It's beautiful.

Dave's a good kisser, a really good one.

I put my head on his shoulder.

He kisses my hair.

I turn and we kiss again.

I can hear a car pull up in the driveway. "My dad's home."

Dave stands up, grabs my hand, and pulls me up.

My father makes a lot of noise opening the door, more than usual.

"Hi, Dad." I realize that Dave and I are still holding hands.

"Hello, Mr. Brooks." Dave brushes his hair back into place.

My father runs his hand over his bald spot.

Men must have a real thing about hair, sort of like the story about Samson and Delilah.

My father looks at us and smiles. "How about some tea or hot chocolate?"

Dave and I follow him down into the kitchen.

It's a little uncomfortable at first, but soon the three of us are having a good time.

Dad and I tell Dave the saga of Rocky and her babies.

He tells us about the time mice got into the kitchen, and his mother refused to cook another meal until traps were set. Then none of them could stand the sound of the traps snapping, so they put out poison. Gross.

Finally Dave looks at his watch. "I've got to go. My parents said the car had to be back by one o'clock or I can't borrow it again."

We all walk up the steps to the living room. I'm afraid my father's not going to give me a chance to be alone with Dave, but as we get to the door he says, "Good-bye, Boy Scout. See you soon."

I walk out to the car with Dave.

"I've got a feeling that your father came back to check on us." He gives me a kiss.

"He did." I kiss him back. "And if I'm not back in the house in a few minutes, he'll start blinking the porch light off and on."

One last kiss and I go back inside.

My father's sitting in a chair, pretending to read.

I go over to him. "Did you have fun tonight?"

He puts down the paper. "Yes—but I did worry about you. Some days it's not easy being a parent. Not some nights either."

"You don't have to worry," I say.

He looks at me. "You really are growing up."

"I'm still your one and favorite daughter." I hug him.

Hugging my father is definitely not the same as hugging Dave. I guess I am growing up.

When I go to my room, I hear my father dial the phone.

I listen.

He's saying, "She's home safely."

I continue to listen but he's talking softly. It's impossible to hear what he's saying.

I wonder who my father's talking to. I know it's not my mother. Who is he reporting my life to? I don't think I like that. I hope it's not that creep Martha who was at the Expresso. I guess that he just does it because he cares.

As I lie in bed I think about Dave and how I can't see him next weekend because it's Thanksgiving and I've got to be with my mother.

19

Thanksgiving vacation.

One thing I'm thankful for is that Rosie and I got seats on the Divorce Express.

That's more than a lot of people can say.

It's the day before Thanksgiving, and lots of people are going down to the City, more than there are seats. There were even some people left behind, waiting to catch the next bus.

Passengers are standing in the aisle with their suitcases and packages. They'll have to stand all the way to New York. It's a real bummer.

The first real snow of the year is starting to come down.

I'm exhausted. So's Rosie. We went to the school cafeteria meeting last night, and it didn't end till real late. It's hard work, planning nutritional meals on a small school budget. I'm beginning to see why the school had trouble.

Rosie's sound asleep next to me and I keep nodding off. Why did we have to go to school today, even for half a day? It's such a waste. No one really does anything. Half the kids have already left on vacations. The other half just sit around and play Hangman and stuff.

All of a sudden the bus makes a funny sound.

I sit up straight.

So does Rosie.

The bus driver pulls over to the side of the road, just past the end of the New York Thruway. He gets out and checks the bus.

People start yelling, "Oh, no—not this too." "What's going on? I've got to catch another bus after this one." And: "This is the last straw."

The bus driver returns, talks into his radio, and then turns around to make an announcement. "Okay, folks. Sorry for the inconvenience. We've got a flat, and with the weather getting worse, I can't take a chance on driving with it. Another bus is on the way. Just sit tight."

Someone yells, "How the hell do you expect us to sit tight when we're standing?"

"Then stand tight," some wise guy calls out.

The bus driver tries to calm everyone down.

I feel kind of sorry for him. It's his Thanksgiving eve too.

Some people from the front of the bus are trying to work their way to the back to go to the bathroom.

They have to get through the aisles, trying not to step on or push anyone.

The snow's coming down worse.

Rosie says, "Maybe we'll get in so late that my father won't make me go to my grandmother's house tomorrow."

"I didn't know you didn't like her. I don't like mine either. My father's mother. My mother's mother I love."

Rosie says, "I kind of like her, but it's a real mess. She's always making cracks about my mother."

"How can she? Mindy's wonderful." I can't believe it. I think of all the times I've been able to talk to her about all sorts of things.

Rosie shakes her head. "My grandmother doesn't think so. She hates Mindy because she's white and Jewish. And Mindy's family hates my father because he's black and Christian. Me—I'm not only black and white, I'm also Jewish. The whole combination is enough to drive each side a little nuts."

I nod. "My grandmothers get upset because even though both of my parents are Jewish, neither of them practice and they never sent me to any organized religious thing." I look out the window and see that the snow is coming down faster.

Rosie continues. "My life's like a soap opera, only without breaks for commercials. I'm used to it. I've lived with it all my life. And it's always going to be a little like that. Well, at least it's not boring."

The second bus pulls up.

People cheer.

The bus driver tells us not to all pile out at once. It's too cold out and everyone could get sick standing around. Anyway he says that they want to try out some new seating arrangement.

Rosie and I end up sitting next to Stevie, the little kid who throws up a lot. I hope he manages to make it to Port Authority without losing his lunch. It's a little tight, three people in a two-seat place. I think they put us together because we're all pretty skinny. Then they hand us Gina Raymond, five years old and another Divorce Express regular. She sits on my lap.

I hope none of us has to get up to go to the bathroom.

There are still people standing, but not as many. And later they're going to switch places with people who are now sitting. One of the good things about sitting with four people in a two-seat place is that we won't have to get up.

Someone starts singing a Christmas carol. Lots of people join in.

Then Rosie begins a Chanukah song. People join in again.

The bus skids a little.

I hope that Stevie's stomach is okay.

The driver's going very slowly.

One of the high school seniors starts singing "Trees," the regular version. I guess that some of the adults went to Kilmer or just know the song because there are a lot of people singing.

Then Rosie and I start to sing "Cafeteria." The other Kilmer kids join in.

People on the bus laugh and applaud. They start passing out food that they've brought along for the holidays. I contribute the granola cookies my father gave me. We get some great cookies, fruit cake, and pumpkin pie.

The pumpkin pie's so good that I get the recipe for my father. He's going to love it.

The bus creeps along.

On the side of the road I can see cars pulled over.

Gina's fallen asleep. She's got her head on Rosie, her middle on me, and her feet on Stevie and she's sucking her thumb.

The closer we get to New Jersey, the less snow.

It's always worse upstate, at least at first.

Finally we reach the Lincoln Tunnel, go through it, and pull into the Port Authority building.

Stevie hasn't thrown up, something else to be thankful for.

"We're here because we're here because we're here because we're here," everyone sings.

We've been on the bus for four and a half hours, two hours late.

People get off the bus stiffly, like they've been in a rolling sardine can.

We're in the middle of the bus, so it takes awhile for us to get out.

"Free at last," Rosie says as we step off the bus. "I can't believe I've still got a subway to catch."

I hear someone call my name. "Phoebe."

It's my mother. She's got this worried-changing-to-glad look on her face.

She hugs me. "Where's Rosie?"

"Here," Rosie says, raising her hand.

People who go to school raise hands instinctively. I've noticed that.

My mother hugs her even though they've never met before. I guess she's been really nervous. It's the first time since the very beginning that she's met me at the bus.

She stands up, catches her breath, and says, "Rosie, you are to spend the night with us."

"Yay," Rosie and I both say at the same time.

My mother continues. "Your father has to work late, and your stepmother couldn't leave her children to wait for you. It's too late and dangerous for you to get downtown by yourself. Your parents and I've decided that staying with us is best. Your father will pick you up tomorrow morning."

Rosie and I look at each other and smile. It's all arranged. Somehow they've all been talking.

As we gather up our suitcases my mother says, "You two know all the kids who ride the bus alone. Are any of them not being met by their parents? It's not safe for them to be here alone. Let's make sure they're all right."

That's like my mother. Sometimes she can think only of herself. Other times she can really come through.

She checks it out, in a very logical way. That's like my mother too—superorganized and take-charge personality. Once she sees that everyone's accounted for, she says, "Time to go. Anyone hungry?"

"Starved," Rosie and I both say at the same time. I've noticed that happens a lot with friends. You get to the point when you start to say things together or sometimes not even have to say some things out loud.

"Okay." My mother pulls back her hair. "We'll get some food as soon as we call your father and Rosie's parents. When the snow started to come down so hard and the weather reports predicted problems, we made these plans."

"I'll call Daddy," I say.

"And I'll call my parents," Rosie says.

My mother walks to the phone booth with us. "Rosie, call your father first." When Rosie finishes talking, my mother says, "You don't have to call your mother's house. She and Jim said that no matter how late it is, to call Phoebe's father's house. That's where they'll both be."

No matter how late it is, they'll both be there—at the same place.

I look at Rosie.

She looks at me.

My mother looks at both of us.

Finally my mother picks up the phone, dials Wood-stock, and tells them we're safe.

Rosie and I each talk to our parents.

Neither of us asks what they're doing together, no matter how late it is.

I want to talk to Rosie about what's going on . . . and I bet she wants to talk to me about it.

It's not a good idea in front of my mother.

I can't wait until Rosie and I are alone.

20

We're finally going to get a chance to talk.

It was so hard sitting through dinner with my mother when all I wanted to do was talk to Rosie about Mindy and my father.

Somehow it didn't seem like a wise move to bring up the subject in front of my mother.

Now we're alone. Or at least we will be as soon as Rosie gets out of the bathroom.

I look around my room. It's pink and frilly and kind of preppy-looking. Everything's in place and doesn't show much personality.

My room in Woodstock is different. During the time I've lived there, the room has changed from when it was just a summer place. There are pictures all over the walls, candles, stained-glass pieces on the window. It feels like it's mine.

This room in the City doesn't feel like the me I've become.

I think about my father and Rosie's mother. Is it possible? What's the story? Are they going out? Was Mindy the person he called to say I was home safely from my date? Is my father the person that Rosie thinks is making her mother so happy or were they just worried about us and decided to worry together?

Why didn't they tell us? I thought my father and I had a deal to discuss important things like this.

Rosie returns, toothbrush in hand.

"Do you think our parents are going out with each other?" I ask her.

She flops down on the lower part of my trundle bed. "I was thinking about that while I flossed my teeth. I think they are. Something strange is definitely going on. Usually when Mindy starts going out with someone, she tells me. This time she's said nothing."

"My father hasn't either." I bite my fingernail.

"Are you upset?" Rosie asks. "I think it's great. I like your father. We would really be sisters if they were together."

"That part's great," I agree. "And I like Mindy a lot. It's just hard to think of him involved with anyone."

"We could ask them," she says, fluffing up her pillow. "Anyway you're going out with Dave now and in a couple of years you'll be going away to college. Your father's going to have to make his own life. That's the kind of stuff that Mindy and I talk about."

"Do you think I could be jealous?" That sounds right as I say it.

"Maybe," Rosie says. "Fathers and daughters. I know I have trouble with my stepmother. Maybe that's part of it."

It's definitely something to think about.

Rosie puts the blanket around her body and yawns. "Let's get some sleep."

"You can go to sleep soon," I promise. "But first let's talk a little more. They probably are spending the night together. Can you imagine our parents—"

"Doing it?" Rosie finishes my thought. "I don't want to think about it right now."

I touch the satin part of my blanket just like I did when I was little. "Do you think they're serious?"

"You keep asking for answers to things that we're not even sure are questions. Maybe, if it is, they'll decide to live together. If they do, we won't have to keep trading the unicorn shirt back and forth. It'll stay in the same house." Rosie lies down.

I decide to let her go to sleep. "I'll keep quiet now."

"Thanks, pal." She pulls the cover over her head. "I do have one question. . . . Your father doesn't really believe much in religion, does he?"

"Not the organized kind," I answer.

"My grandparents will really love that," she says from under the pillow.

After I turn out the light, I stare at the ceiling. There is still a fluorescent universe pasted up there. Before the divorce my father helped me put up all the little pieces. When the light goes out, all the planets, stars, moons, and sun shine.

I think about the world—the one on the ceiling . . . the one in New York . . . and the one in Woodstock.

I've always kind of thought of myself as the sun—the one that all of the others revolved around.

It's not true, I guess. It feels like someone's ripped the sun out of place but everything is going along anyway.

I sure hope that I'm still part of everything. If my father is going out with Mindy, that means that he'll want to spend more time with her and do more things together. I won't have him to myself.

Maybe it won't be bad, but it sure will be different.

How can Rosie take the whole thing so calmly?

I wish I could.

21

Rosie's gone.

Her father just picked her up.

He seemed okay. It's hard to tell the first time I meet someone. I just kept remembering how he acts to Mindy.

Mindy. My father.

I have to deal with my mother at the moment. That's enough to think about.

I go into the kitchen.

My mother's sitting at the table, drinking another cup of coffee.

Pouring a glass of milk, I join her.

She asks me whether Dad and Mindy are going out, kind of casually, but in a way that I know she's really interested.

I shrug. Even if I knew, I wouldn't say anything. I've learned not to get in the middle.

Then she says, "Phoebe, remember how upset I was when Duane and I broke up?"

Remember? How can I forget? That's all she's talked about lately.

Continuing, she says, "One of the problems was that we never could spend much time together when you visited. I didn't want you to get upset because he wanted to stay here, and I know it made you uncomfortable. But now Duane and I have talked it out and I want you to get to know him better . . . to like each other. He's very important to me and I want to continue the relationship. He wants to be with me and I want to be with him."

The phone rings.

It's for her. . . . Duane.

While she's talking to him, I make my getaway.

Going into my room, I want to tear everything apart.

How can she say that I've got to do something that I can't?

I pick up a stuffed animal and throw it across the room.

It hits the wall.

I pick it up and hug it to me. "I'm sorry."

I'm not sure if I'm sorrier for my stuffed animal or for me.

When my mother gets off the phone, I call Dave.

Something in my life has to stay the same.

I hope that he still cares.

I call him.

He still does care, a lot, he says.

I'm really glad that I don't have to depend on my parents for everything.

22

My opinion of Duane hasn't changed.

I have to sit at a Thanksgiving dinner at a restaurant, watching the two of them and pretending to listen.

I can't believe that she's picked him, that he's so important to her.

He is though. I can tell. My mother acts like Sunshine Anderson when she's around Duane. Sunshine is this kid in my homeroom who is really good at lots of things, sports and schoolwork. But when she's around her boyfriend, Ray, she acts like she can't do anything. That's what my mother's doing. I know that she can do lots of stuff by herself, but when she's with Duane, she lets him make all the decisions. And he treats her like a precious china doll.

Maybe it's the difference in their ages. She's thirty-six. He's forty-eight, almost half a century old.

I just don't understand it.

The waiter brings dessert: pumpkin pie.

Duane starts talking to me about his children. "For a while Duane junior wanted to be a musician, but now he's found himself and he's in business with me."

"If he'd stayed a musician, would you have said that he'd found himself or would he have been lost?" I ask, taking my fork and stabbing it into my pumpkin pie.

The pie's lousy, not half as good as the piece I had on the bus. I'm beginning to think that everything about Woodstock is better.

My mother flashes me a warning look.

I've gotten to him. I can tell.

He frowns and says, "No. The arts are all right if you can make big money, but most people can't. Let Duane junior's music be a hobby. People have responsibilities to meet."

I think about the wonderful painting my father's doing. Doesn't he have a responsibility to pursue that talent? He thinks so. So do I. I stab my pie again, pretending that it's Duane senior.

He continues. "My daughter, Beatrice, is very happy. She's married to an orthopedic surgeon and has a beautiful daughter, with another baby on the way."

Two thoughts enter my brain at the same time. Duane's a grandfather. My mother is going out with a grandfather who wants to stay overnight with her. I didn't even think that grandfathers had sex anymore. I also think how much I want to tell him that my father goes to a chiropractor, that he's nervous about the traditional medical profession.

Looking at my mother, I can see how tense she is getting, so I decide not to say anything.

Sometimes I think that I spend more time protecting my mother's feelings than she does protecting mine.

Duane turns to her and says, "Honey. Don't forget. Sometime this weekend, I want you to go for your fitting."

My mother nods, smiles, and then explains to me. "Duane's already picked out my Christmas present. It's a mink coat."

She just bought herself a sable coat. How many creatures have to die for my mother? That does it.

I say, "My father and I think that killing animals for fashion is barbaric and unnecessary."

"Dreamers. Idealists." Duane pats me on the hand. "Don't you wear shoes with leather?"

I can see that my mother's really upset.

I hope that every time she wears that stupid coat, she thinks of this talk, so she can never totally enjoy it.

Duane pays for the meal and we leave the restaurant. The doorman gets us a taxi.

As we head toward home I hear Duane say, "Don't worry, dear. We can work this problem out."

So now I'm a problem.

What makes me angriest is that my mother doesn't even defend me.

When we get back to the apartment, Duane says

good night to me. I go into my room and shut the door. They're mumbling out there.

My mother walks in a few minutes later and says, "We've got to talk."

"There's nothing to say."

"Yes, there is." She's very upset. "I want you and Duane to get along. It's very important to me. You are both very important parts of my life."

"Why do you have to act that way with him . . . like he's right about things?"

"Because I think he is most of the time. Just because he doesn't agree with your views doesn't make him wrong."

"Why choose him?" I want to know.

"Look, Phoebe. When I married your father, I thought he had the same views I did, that he wanted the same things out of life that I did. Well, he didn't . . . but Duane does. I'm sure of that. If you don't like a lot of what Duane thinks, then you don't like a lot of what I think."

"I don't understand how you can like him," I say.

"Well, I do. I love him. And you don't have to understand. You just have to accept it."

"What if I don't want to?"

"Then you've got a real problem."

"So do you." I try to stare her down.

She stares back. "I seem to have a problem no matter what. All day long I'm in charge of a lot of people. I make important decisions. It's a lot of responsibility, which I like. However, when I come home, I don't like to walk into an empty house. I want someone to care about me, hear about my day, go out to dinner. You're not here to do that . . . and anyway, even if you were, Duane would still be important to me. He's a nice man. He respects my opinions. We go out and have fun."

"You also like his money." I sneer at her.

She looks like I've slapped her. Then she gets angry. "You selfish little brat. You certainly like having money, too, and the things it can buy. . . . Let me tell you something—I make enough to support myself well. A good thing too—since your father certainly isn't in any position to help. . . . Yes, Duane does have a lot of money. That's nice, but it's not everything. He offers me love and caring and companionship. He also wants things to be good with you. But you refuse to see that. Since you've moved to Woodstock, you've changed so much, I hardly know you. It's like you're always judging me and everything and everyone about me. And there's no way for me to win."

Her saying that makes me feel bad. I don't know whether I was right or wrong about what I said about the money. All I know is that I don't like Duane, and she's choosing him instead of me. And why does everything with her have to be either winning or losing? I hope that I'm not like her.

My parents are so different, and yet I'm a part of both of them. It's so hard to know what I want, what I think.

She looks at me. "I care about you a lot, Phoebe. You're not fair. Give this a chance."

She says I'm not fair. What about her?

As she walks out the door she says, "Duane will be staying here tonight. I don't want to hear one unpleasant word out of your mouth."

I stare as she leaves.

Maybe she's right. . . . I have changed since I moved. But I'm not so sure it's as bad as she thinks.

This is definitely a Thanksgiving Day that I'm not going to forget.

It could be worse.

I could be a turkey.

23

I'm trying to like Duane. I really am, I think, as the three of us ride to Port Authority.

I even made a list of his positive points: He doesn't smoke cigars. . . . He doesn't pick his nose. . . . He loves his grandchild. . . . He's not a mugger. . . . He really loves my mother.

He's just not my kind of person. Nothing's wrong with hunting as a sport, he says. Even my mother agrees with me about that. The cafeteria actions were wrong, he tells me. "Children should be seen, not heard." Also he hates it when people show emotion.

It was hard waking up in the morning knowing that I was going to see Duane at the breakfast table.

It's worse knowing it's going to be a permanent situation.

They're going to get married.

My mother and Grandpa Duane are "tying the knot."

I hope they tie the knot around each other's throats.

Doesn't she care at all what I think, how I feel?

The man's a real creep.

I hate him.

We arrive at Port Authority and go down to my bus. Rosie's already there.

Duane's trying to be so nice to me. "Let us know when you get your Christmas list made up. The things your father can't afford, we'll get for you."

I'd like to put a hit man on that list, one that would do away with Duane. . . . The things that my father can't afford. He makes it sound like my father's a real failure. Well, I'd like to see Duane paint, or consider my feelings the way my father does. That would show him who the real failure is.

I hate Duane. I think I even hate my mother. Not totally. I mean, she is my mother and all that, but I really don't like her much.

My mother looks so happy, I could throw up. How can she be so happy about something that's going to make me so miserable?

When they told me last night that they were getting married next month, they also let me know that they'd be living in Duane's apartment and selling ours after it goes co-op. She can make a good profit on it.

Selling our place, the apartment I'd lived in since I was born, where I come to now.

They'll be living in a luxury building on Sutton Place. I guess lots of people would be happy about a move like that, but I'm not. I know our neighborhood, the doormen, a lot of the people. Even though I'm only in New York part-time, I don't feel like it's strange territory. Now I'm really going to feel like a visitor, not a real part of my mother's life.

It's going to be very strange. I'm going to have to go to an apartment that I won't feel at home in to be with a stepfather I hate (Plastic Pop, I've started calling him in my head) and deal with a mother who thinks only of herself.

In the beginning I used to make lots of excuses for her because she was my mother. I guess the truth is that if she were just some person on the street, I wouldn't want to know her, but she's my mother. And the court's given her joint custody.

I wonder what would happen if I refused to see her, whether I would have to go to jail?

My mother says, as I'm getting on the bus, "Next time you come down, we'll pick out your dress for the wedding."

I rush up the bus steps.

If I say anything to her, it will be to suggest that I wear black.

Rosie follows.

She arrived just in time to hear the end of our conversation.

I throw my bag in the overhead rack, sit in a seat, and start to cry. I hate that. I cry when I'm angry. At least that's better than my mother, who cries when she wants something.

Rosie says, "Are they really getting married?"

I nod and sniffle.

She shakes her head. "At least I had awhile to get

used to my father and his wife. Wow, that's a real shock for you. Do you think they have to get married, that your mother's pregnant?"

My mother pregnant, having to get married, that would really be something. "She wouldn't have any more kids. She told me that once." I shake my head. "She said it's because she and Duane are old-fashioned, that they don't believe in living together without being married, that it wouldn't look good for their businesses. What hypocrites. He can spend the night, but they can't live together without marriage."

Rosie says, "Look, maybe it won't be so terrible."

So terrible. I tell her about the mink coat . . . Duane junior . . . having to move out of my apartment. . . .

Rosie says, "I've got an idea. Since you're stuck with the situation, why not make the best of it? Why don't you give him a Christmas list of everything you've ever wanted?"

I think about that. It would be fun, except then I'd owe him, be indebted. No way.

Rosie continues. "Some people say divorce kids are lucky. We get chances to travel, different places to visit, more presents. I don't think it's always so easy for us. It's rough sometimes."

I agree. "You go to school in one place, but when there are special events like dances, parties, games, and events, you've got to miss them because you have to visit the other parent. There are always two places to live, to keep clean. I tried so hard for things to be nice and easy. When both parents needed me to keep them company, I was there."

Both of us sit quietly, thinking about all this stuff.

I remember how awful it was for me when they first separated. Then when they got the divorce. Then there was the move to the country, but that turned out well. I have friends, especially Rosie. And Dave's real special to me, my first real kind of grown-up caring about someone who isn't in my family. So I have survived some rough stuff. I guess I'll make it through this too.

Maybe Duane's got so much money, he can have his computer company build a Robot Daughter, one who visits weekends and holidays and does everything they want, without being a "problem."

It's so rotten. That's the only way it's going to work out the way they want. I'm just never going to be the kind of daughter she wants, not if I'm going to be the kind of person I want to be.

Actually I think I've come up with a great idea. Rent A Robot Family. The slogan could be "We try hardest—the nuts and bolts of families." People could rent whichever family member is the hardest to deal with, and the robots could be programmed to do exactly what you want. Then the real people could go on being exactly what they are and it wouldn't make a difference.

It's pretty sad when you think about it, wanting machines to be something people can't be.

24

"The dynamic duo awaits us," Rosie says, looking out the window when the bus stops at the Village Green.

Mindy and my father are holding up a sign that says WELCOME HOME, PHOEBE AND ROSIE.

As soon as they realize that we've seen it they turn the sign around. That sign says WELCOME HOME, ROSIE AND PHOEBE.

"No favoritism allowed," Rosie says. "Equal billing. Those two are really something."

"They are. Something special." I feel much better.

We grab our bags and leave the bus.

Mindy and my father look so proud of themselves.

The sign is put down as they reach out to hug us.

I rush into my father's arms and start to cry.

Holding me, he keeps asking what's wrong.

Rosie fills him in.

"When we get to the house, I'll pick up my car, and Rosie and I will go home to give you and Phoebe a chance to talk." Mindy touches my father's arm and runs her fingers through my hair.

We get into the car and drive back to the house. My father keeps reaching over and patting my hand as he drives.

I feel like I've been on a dangerous space-shuttle ride and I've splashed down safely.

As the car is parked in our driveway I say, "Mindy. Rosie. Stay. I want you to."

"If you're sure," Mindy says.

"I'm sure."

Going into the living room, I sit down on the couch and wrap myself in a quilt.

My father puts some logs in the stove and sits down next to me.

Mindy's sitting on the rocker and Rosie's cross-legged on the floor.

"I'm okay," I say. "I'm sorry I made a scene."

"Don't be sorry," my father says. "You've got a right to your feelings."

I start crying again. All weekend I've tried to keep my feelings closed up inside. When I tried to show them to my mother, she wouldn't let me. So now they're all coming out at once.

My father hugs me and rocks me back and forth like he did when I was little.

I calm down. Taking a deep breath, I tell them about the upcoming marriage, how I hate Duane, how I don't want to go to New York anymore.

They all listen quietly.

"So," I say, concluding, "they can both rot in hell. I'm never going to see them again."

"Never's a long time," my father says. "It does sound rough though. Look, I'll give your mother a call and explain that you're upset and that you and she should talk about it."

"Did it work when you tried to explain to her what you were upset about? Were you able to work it out?" I ask.

He shakes his head. "I see your point. Sometimes I think you and I are so much alike that your mother can't handle the things in you that are like me. Maybe that's one of the problems."

"Maybe." I crawl further into the quilt. "But it's awful when she won't listen to me."

"Did you listen to her?" my father asks.

"I tried . . . but not about Duane."

"That's a big but. Duane's going to be her husband . . . your stepfather," he says. "How do you think she feels when you say awful things about him? Wouldn't you feel terrible if I refused to give Dave a chance when he arrived on the scene—even though it was hard for me to see you with someone else?"

"That's different," I say.

"All I ask is that you think about the situation. No matter what, Duane is going to be in your life."

"You wouldn't like him either," I say.

My father thinks about that for a minute. "You may be right . . . but I'm going to have to learn to deal with him too. He and I may have to talk about what the three of you plan for the time you stay with your mother. . . . Divorce and remarriage means having more people in your life. There's no way around it."

"It's not always easy though," Mindy says.

Rosie says, "I'll second that."

"I realize that," my father says. "Phoebe, just think about it. Your mother *is* marrying Duane. How you act now is going to affect what it's like later. You have some control of that."

"Does that mean I have to lie and pretend?" I make a face.

"What do you think?" my father asks.

It's quiet for a while. I can hear the wood burning.

Finally I say, "I have to learn how to handle this new situation so that it works out well for me . . . as well as it can without it being what I really want. That's it, isn't it?"

He smiles.

"It's not easy," I say.

"I know." He hugs me. "But I have faith in you."

I'm glad he does. I'm not so sure I do.

I say, "Thanks. I feel better now. I'll think about it."

We sit quietly.

Finally I say, "Look. I really do feel better now. I'm even hungry."

"Good." Mindy starts to get up. "Let's get the dinner on the table."

"Not so fast." Rosie grabs her sleeve.

Mindy sits down.

Rosie continues, as if she's interrogating them, like in the old war movies. "You will be so kind as to tell us exactly what has been going on behind our backs. We want names, dates, and other pertinent information. We have ways to make you talk, you know."

I join in. "Rosie, should we stick bamboo shoots under their fingernails . . . or drip water on their heads . . . or use the dreaded tickle torture?"

"The tickle torture it is." She jumps on my father, and I grab Mindy from behind.

Neither of our parents can stand being tickled.

We really get them.

Soon we're all rolling all over the floor laughing.

When we calm down, I say, "Come on now, tell us. When we called, how come you were both here and planning to be here till all hours and now are still together several days later? Tell us. We're allowed to see R-rated movies. We can handle this."

My father and Mindy are smiling at each other.

He begins. "Mindy and I have been going out since the first time we met."

"How come you never told us? I feel betrayed." I let him know.

"We decided to wait and see if it was serious." Mindy puts her hand in my father's. "If it didn't work out, we didn't want to tell either of you."

"Why not?" Rosie asks.

"Neither of us wanted either of you to feel uncomfortable in each other's home. We know what good friends you are, and we didn't want to do anything that would cause you to take sides or be upset." Rosie and I look at each other.

"Now we know it is serious," my father breaks in. "That we care about each other and it's time for you to know, to be part of our relationship. That's why we asked you to come back early to discuss it. We plan to keep going out. We know that will affect both of you."

"We had no idea that Phoebe's mother was going to announce her marriage and the move," Mindy says. "We wouldn't have hit you with all of this at once. It's almost too much."

I nod, then say, "So what's the deal? Are we going to all live together? Are we going to have a baby brother or sister?"

"Bite your tongue," Mindy says. "No more babies."

"Not for me either. I'm happy with the child I have. And with Rosie too," my father says.

"Thanks." I hug him. "Just don't love Rosie more than me."

"Sibling rivalry already," Rosie says. "It's just what we're studying in Family Living class."

"Don't rush us. We're just going out, getting to know each other," Mindy says.

"So how do you both feel?"

There's quiet as Rosie and I think about it.

I say, "Does this mean you're going steady? I approve."

"Me too," Rosie says.

We talk some more.

With my mother there's no talk. With my father sometimes it seems like there's almost too much.

When we get up to have dinner, Mindy and my father hug and kiss each other. I realize that over the whole weekend, I never saw Duane and my mother show any real affection, other than calling each other "dear" and "honey."

Finally we sit down to have our second turkey dinner of the weekend.

The phone rings.

It's Dave. He asks if I'd like to go out and make out with him.

I like a guy who knows his own mind.

"I'd love to." I giggle. "But we've got company, Rosie and Mindy."

He laughs. "Well, they can watch."

I say, "I don't think that's a family activity." As I say it I think of how easy it is to think of us as a family.

He says, "I would really just like to see you. Do you think we can arrange that?"

I ask my father if Dave can come over after dinner.

After checking with Mindy and Rosie, he says, "Invite the Boy Scout over. He can join us for dinner."

25

I'm going to the wedding.

Dad thought I should go.

So did Mindy.

And Rosie.

And Dave.

Even I think I should go. After all, how many times will I get the chance to go to my own mother's wedding? . . . I hope only once.

I still think Duane's a drip, but he does care about my mother and makes her happy. That counts for something.

He's even letting me redecorate the room that will be mine when I visit. I won't have to use the furniture from our old apartment. He did cringe, though, when I put the I ♥ WOODSTOCK sticker on the door, but he didn't say anything.

Dave promised to be my date. I think that the main reason he's going along is to make sure that I don't throw poisoned rice at the bridal couple.

I've even decided not to send Duane and my mother the sympathy card I bought. I'll pick out a wedding card. It's not easy though to find one that says HAPPY WEDDING, MOM AND PLASTIC POP.

I know that when I go to the wedding, I'm going to think of my father and how he's doing back in Woodstock. I bet it's not easy for him, especially since his own mother's going to the wedding. Sometimes I not only dislike Grandmother Brooks, I also don't understand her—or my mother for inviting her.

I've decided to keep riding the Divorce Express even though I'm not sure it's going to work out. My mother and I sat down and made a deal to come only every other weekend so that I can go out with Dave and be with the rest of my friends.

I don't feel entrapped anymore, with no place to go. I have both of my parents' places . . . and I'm learning to have my own place in the world.

I've learned something else too. If you take the letters in the word DIVORCES and rearrange them, they spell DISCOVER.